AN
ODD BIRD

OF THE WING

P.K. BUTLER

PINCHEY HOUSE PRESS
Gettysburg, Pennsylvania, USA

This is a work of fiction. Names, characters, places, and incidents are either products of the author's imagination or are used fictionally. Any resemblance to actual persons, living or dead, events, or locales is entirely coincidental.

PINCHEY HOUSE PRESS
1805 Mummasburg Road
Gettysburg, PA 17325

First published in the United States of America by Pinchey House Press as *The Legend Awakes* (2010, 2008) in the trilogy *Of the Wing*.

3rd Edition, Revised
Copyright © 2021, 2010, 2008 P.K. Butler
All rights reserved

Summary: Claire, an eleven-year-old who can summon birds, meets an old man who roams the forest with his pet chicken. Through their friendship, Claire awakens to an almost mythical hawk with whom she must communicate to learn the secret of her destiny as a champion for birds. Set in north-central Pennsylvania.

ISBN 978-0-9820342-3-1

Library of Congress Control Number: 2020920530

Cover Art by Madli Silm

Printed in the United States of America

The publisher does not have any control over and does not assume any responsibility for third-party Web sites or their content.

For

David

". . . a story combining ecological awareness with mysticism, the themes nicely linked by the mythic role of birds as spiritual messengers."

Kirkus Reviews

Table of Contents

1 Hawk 1
2 Strange Encounters 5
3 Lunatics and Bullies 9
4 Red-Belly and the Wolf Spider 14
5 Save the Beagle 19
6 Chasing the Chicken Man 24
7 A Horrible Discovery 30
8 Moon Woman 37
9 Midnight Rescue 41
10 Call of the Barred Owl 46
11 Campfire Companions 49
12 Earth Magic 54
13 Becky and Her Boyfriend 59
14 Defending Her Own 65
15 The Missed Call 71
16 Lost in the Snow 75
17 One Survives 80
18 The Glass Eye 86
19 Search for the Snowy Owl 90
20 Embers and Ash 95
21 Exposed 100
22 A Chickadee Cheats Death 104
23 Matter of Mind 108
24 Wizard or What? 113

25 Sky Dancing	116
26 Foiled Abduction	118
27 Hallway Hustle	121
28 Dangerous Drunk	125
29 Sitting Target	130
30 Cryptic Answers	135
31 Into the Now	138
32 All That Live	141
33 The Hatchling	146
About the Author	151

1
Hawk

Claire Belle walked briskly through the woods, binoculars hanging from a strap around her neck. She was a birder, a person with a passion for birds. Every day she had a mission: to see, hear, and identify as many birds as possible. Tiny ruby-throated hummingbirds or majestic golden eagles, birds revealed to Claire a mysterious and beautiful world. She reveled in this world that most people, sadly, could not inhabit. For most people did not bother to notice their feathered neighbors. Not so Claire. She was driven to seek them because birds held the answer to a question boiling in her blood: *Who—or what—am I?*

Claire was different from other eleven-year-old girls. She stood a head taller than most, with white hair cropped close to her head. Snow-white lashes, thick and long, trimmed the lids of her yellow-gold eyes, the color of a great horned owl's. In fact, many different animals shared her eye color but no people. And Claire preferred the company of animals, especially birds. In fact, she was obsessed with them. She listened for the songs of chickadees outside her bedroom windows. She searched the sky for hawks and trees for owls. She studied the stripes of sparrows in field guides, listened to recordings of warblers' songs, and kept a daily log of every bird she saw or heard. Hers was the passion of a birder but a breed above, because Claire was somehow related to birds. She didn't know, however, the nature of her relationship. Did she share bird DNA, or was her tie spiritual? Or both? The birds themselves held the answer, and they were trying to tell her. She simply couldn't understand.

Trotting in front of Claire was Sammy, a black-and-white sheepdog. He was her constant companion in daily explorations of the forests surrounding their rural property in north-central Pennsylvania. Soon they were to a yellow birch, or as Claire called it, the Golden Tree. Its satin trunk glistened gold in the late afternoon sun. "Sammy, look!" She pointed to a sugar maple blazing with red and orange leaves. "I found you under that tree when you were just a puppy, lost and hungry." Sammy didn't listen, intent on grazing the ground with his big black nose, searching for a fresh scent. He found one, snorting to trace its track.

"Sammy!" she called, but it was too late. He charged over the low-flowing creek, through the trees, and up the ridge. She could never have caught up and so sat beneath the Golden Tree to wait for his return. Meanwhile, she would look for porcupines hiding high in the trees and listen for fall migrating sparrows heading south for the winter. In an open area among the birch and hemlock trees, she saw a green garter snake, as thick as a fat pencil, glistening like a gem. Studying it through binoculars, she heard a muffled thumping and felt a warm pulse of air against her cheek. She didn't see the red-tailed hawk swooping down from the sky until its talons plucked the snake from the ground. The hawk was huge, like a prehistoric bird. Its dark brown eyes stared from beneath protruding brows directly into her own. Claire could see their expanding pupils, could feel their tug upon her own. She dropped the binoculars, watching the bird's massive, thrashing wings. A splash of cinnamon formed a cross on its creamy chest. Lifting skyward with its struggling prey, the hawk rose above the treetops, its red tail aglow in the sun.

She stood, thoughtless, staring into the blue circle of sky, inhabiting now—without past or future. The external world moved through time without her. Moments passed before she could break the spell cast by the hawk. Only then did she remember Sammy. Where was he? Beyond the ridge over which he had vanished stood the home of the property owner, an old woman who did not like trespassers. The old woman might hear if she hollered for him. So instead she called as a barred owl, a call Sammy knew well since Claire made it so often. The call of the barred owl was the first she learned because it was easy to remember—who cooks for you; who cooks for you all.

"Hoo hoo ho-ho, hoo hoo ho-hooooaw," she hooted toward the ridge, a call her mother had taught her the year her father died, when she was only three. From deep in the woods, a stocky, round-headed barred owl answered her call.

Hoo hoo ho-ho, hoo hoo ho-hooooaw . . .

Printed on Claire's sweatshirt was the owl's image, but she longed to actually see one in the flesh. In a daily log she had entered many calls of the owl but not one sighting. Yet she was determined. From behind came the sound of panting. There stood Sammy, dripping with water, his tail dragging a branch complete with twigs and leaves. She struggled to untangle the branch from his wet fur, curled into spirals and smelling like creek mud. A sudden wind gust blew a shower of yellow leaves through the air and with them the sweet, musky scent of autumn. Some leaves floated to the ground. Others nestled as ornaments within the feathery branches of the evergreens.

Beneath one such hemlock, someone sat, partly hidden behind a low skirting of branches. The man awaited discovery, if not by the strangely pale girl, then by the dog, who certainly would smell him: a seventy-year-old man, five days without a bath. But neither girl nor dog knew they were being watched while the man waited, stroking a gray-and-white beard.

2
Strange Encounters

The sound of a clucking bird filled the afternoon air. Sammy bounded toward the sound, away from the creek and up the hill. Claire hurried behind, huffing with effort, until she reached Sammy's side. The dog barked at something perched in the hemlock tree—a reddish-brown hen! *Whatever is a chicken doing in the middle of the woods?* wondered Claire. Sammy began to growl.

"He don't like me, I guess," said a gruff voice. Claire gasped to see a man sitting beneath the tree. Sammy snarled.

"Tell him it's okay. Else I'll have to climb the tree with my chicken."

Confused, Claire looked from the man to Sammy to the perched chicken.

"That's your chicken?" she asked.

"Her name's Becky. She's a Rhode Island Red."

A tumble of gray-and-white hair, coarse and somewhat kinky, hung about his face. Through strands of it she could barely see the old man's eyes. He wore faded denim overalls and a dingy shirt of long underwear. He didn't scare her because he had a pet chicken.

"I'm Claire; this is Sammy."

"Hello, Claire. My name is Jerry," said the man, standing no taller than she. "Can you leash that dog?" His voice was as crusty as his appearance. "I don't want him to tear into Becky. A hawk did that once already."

"A hawk?" Claire looked with interest at the hen, bobbing

its head as if to say, *Yes, indeed.* "What kind of hawk?" She snapped a leash to Sammy's collar.

Jerry patted his shoulder and the hen flew from a hemlock branch to a padded patch of suede, like a saddle, slung over it. Sammy sprang toward the hen but was yanked back. He strained hard toward the bird, but Claire held firm. Whimpering, Sammy sat again.

"Walk a bit with me, and I'll tell you the story."

Claire and Sammy followed Jerry through the trees.

"Becky wasn't much more than a yearling when it happened," he began. "She was outside the cabin scratching, and I was inside." He stopped to look Claire straight in the eyes. Startled, she looked downward, a lifelong habit to conceal their color, though they were now concealed behind blue-tinted contacts. "Now, some hawks will eat a chicken—"

"Cooper's hawks like chickens," she chirped, looking up again. "And I just saw a red-tail—" She turned to point to the spot below but then stopped. "Wait, you must have seen it, too!"

"That I did." Jerry squinted hard, straining her image through the slits of his eyes. The girl's white hair and thick, long lashes were startling, yet beautiful, like some snow princess in a fairy tale. "And would you believe it? That hawk we just saw was the very same that grabbed my Becky a few years back."

"No!"

"Yes, indeed! The very same one."

But Claire was suspicious. She paused as warnings against talking to strange men filled her mind. But this man was old. She could easily outrun him. Besides, Sammy would protect her. She challenged him. "You were too far away to see him up close."

"See her." The old man raised a bushy eyebrow. "She's no common red-tail, or didn't you notice?" He stroked the hen's downy chest. "That day I heard squawking, and out the window saw a huge hawk wrestling her." Becky bobbed her head excitably while Sammy sifted the air for her scent, his large wet nose rising higher and higher, as if pulled by a string.

"I threw a feather-down pillow to knock that hawk off balance." Here Jerry halted, pointing in the distance, as if the scene he described were etched in the air. "After collecting herself, she stuck her talons into the pillow and dragged it along the ground for a bit until releasing it to sail into the sky."

Claire giggled.

"It was funny, but don't laugh yet. You forget about Becky." The path they followed connected to an old logging road, scattered with freshly fallen green acorns. "When I got her, poor thing, she was sliced from chest to belly." The hen pecked at Jerry's beard. "I kept some whiskey at the cabin. You know it disinfects, right? I poured it right along that cut. Becky should've howled in pain, but she didn't, being that close to death. Then I got out my needle and thread and stitched her up just like I was sewing a quilt."

Both gazed at Becky, the hen who survived a hawk attack and a sewing kit. But neither noticed Sammy's keen interest in the hen. The dog walked behind Jerry, still loosely held by a leash. When Becky ruffled her feathers, Sammy sprang but then collided with Jerry's outstretched arm. The dog dropped to the ground, winded. Jerry stared hard at the dog, with not a sign of regret. "Girl, you should train your dog better."

Crouching over her hurt dog, Claire suddenly felt scared. The man towering over her seemed less old and more threatening. "I think you hurt him."

"He's winded is all," he said and spit on the ground. "But

I'll tell you one thing. That dog won't soon again try for my Becky." At this point, Becky fluttered to the ground, proving Jerry correct. Head now propped on Claire's lap, Sammy simply stared at the strutting hen through woeful eyes.

Claire brooded over his dismissal of her dog though mindful he was trying to protect Becky. Even so, something was wrong in what he did. "You shouldn't have hurt him," she said, expecting some word of regret. But the old man offered none.

"I never seen two such sorrowful pups," he said. "Get up and get home." In response, Claire and Sammy bounced off the ground to watch the man march off, his hen scampering after.

At supper, Claire didn't dare tell her mother about Jerry. In bed that night, the mystery of the bearded old man kept her awake. She gazed endlessly at the full moon suspended in her window, flooding her room with white light. On a bedside rug, Sammy lay on his back, his shaggy legs suspended. Claire stroked his white chest as he pedaled the air, running somewhere in his sleep. She stuffed the pillow under her chin and gazed at the moon's silver trail across their still pond. A ripple ran across the water's smooth black surface; the light trail sparkled and flashed. At the pond's far edge, a small dog was lapping a large drink. Claire grabbed her bedside binoculars. It was a beagle. She strained to make sense of some form illuminated in the moonlight beside the animal. A pair of white arms, a bearded face, and overalls—it was Jerry! Astounded, she watched as Jerry urged the dog from the water, and the two disappeared down a steep bank behind the pond and into the surrounding woods.

3
Lunatics and Bullies

Claire stood outside her house, awaiting the school bus. Hers was the only house for a quarter mile, sitting in the middle of a seventeen-acre parcel of land, half which lay on either side of a narrow country road. From the front porch, the view was of wild pasture, bordered on the right by a creek, flowing downstream through hundreds of acres of woodland. It was an adventurous child's paradise, especially if shared with a friend. Claire was looking for that friend in Victor, a boy she had met on the school bus only six weeks before.

Claire scanned the gray soup sky for birds but saw none on the wing, though a flock of goldfinch arrayed itself prettily, like golden pears, in a locust tree beside the white wood-framed house with black shutters. In small clusters the birds descended on the feeder overstuffed with sunflower seeds. Among the flock perched one tufted titmouse, some hundred feet away, but Claire's eyesight was keen. She could easily discern its gray feathers from the olive drab of the wintering finch. Her mother told everyone that her daughter had eyes like a hawk. Of course, her mother meant it as a metaphor, but Claire understood differently.

The school bus groaned to a halt with a belch of fumes and Claire boarded it, empty but for two round-faced twin brothers who always sat in the backseat. They never spoke to her but always stared with obvious interest until she dropped into a seat halfway down the aisle. Several stops later, a smiling boy bounced up the steps, ambled down the aisle, and plopped onto the seat beside her. The smallest boy in Claire's sixth-grade class, Victor was the physical opposite of her in every way. She was tall; Victor was short. She had milk-white hair; Victor's was ink-black. Her skin seemed bleached; Victor's seemed baked to a golden brown. Victor's dark chocolate eyes were creamy and sweet and always made her blush when they sought her fake blue eyes. She quickly looked down and away.

"Why are you always so shy?" he said with a giggle, chasing her face with his own.

Grinning, Claire gently pushed his shoulder away. Eager to change the subject, she tried to tell him of her mysterious encounter, but mention of the old man with a pet chicken caused Victor to shriek, "What did he do to you?!"

Startled, she shouted back, "He didn't do anything to me!"

Twisting in seats, sleepy or talkative students attended to their exchange.

Casting words downward, Victor whispered, "What did he do to Sammy?"

"He didn't do any—" she faltered because the old man had knocked Sammy to the ground.

Victor saw her hesitancy. "What?" he cried, volume again high. "That was the Chicken Man, and he's a lunatic!"

Claire shook her head toward him and the eager onlookers. "Later. Off the bus."

"But Sammy," he insisted.

"He's okay." She shifted her eyes from him to wide-eyed Yolanda, whose chin perched atop the seat back.

"Okay," he said, regaining his poise. "Later."

Claire always had difficulty controlling her emotions, but Victor seldom did. When necessary, he composed himself quickly. She attributed this trait to his father and grandparents, who were full-blooded Cochiti Indians. She thought of indigenous people as more centered because they remained mindful of the Earth. Proud of his heritage, Victor had

Lunatics and Bullies

explained it to her in detail. His grandparents lived on a reservation in New Mexico, where his father, George, had been raised. But his father left the pueblo to go to college, where he met Victor's mother, Rose, a non-native woman. And though Victor was half Native American, he identified himself wholly as one, wearing chokers of bone and leather made for him by his father. And he wore his straight, shiny black hair long, spilling onto his shoulders.

Claire stepped off the bus directly into the path of Billy, a boy with a donkey face. "Bird Girl," he snickered, glancing right and left to see whose ears attended his wit. His right eye hid behind a curtain of limp, brown hair. Everyone knew he called her Bird Girl because every day she wore a T-shirt or sweatshirt stamped with the image of a bird. But no one knew that the birds she wore were certain to cross her path that same day. Today she wore a red-bellied woodpecker.

Though a seventh-grader, Billy stood no taller than she. He blocked her way. Claire wanted to stare him down but couldn't risk exposing her fake-colored eyes. She glanced away.

From behind, Victor stepped up and in a quiet voice said to Billy, "Nobody likes a jerk." Billy's mouth dropped and his one visible eye twitched as he pushed the smaller boy aside to stomp away. Victor turned to Claire and shrugged. "Don't mind him. He's messed up."

But Claire did mind him. Billy gave kids an excuse to stare at her, something they didn't need. Whether she walked down a hallway or the school bus aisle, heads always turned to follow. And with turning heads came the sound of whispers: "Psspsspss . . . her skin's so white it's almost blue . . . psspsspss . . . have you ever seen hair that color . . . psspsspss . . . and why does she wear it like a boy?"

These whisperers didn't know that Claire's hearing was

sharp, like an owl that can hear a mouse scurrying through a burrow under the snow. Years of listening to birds in the woods had honed her hearing. She heard what they said but pretended not to. What they whispered was hurtful yet strangely comforting because no one mentioned her eyes. In that one way, at least, she appeared normal to others.

Turning against the flow of students, Claire looked for Victor, who was no longer behind her. She hurried forward, resigned to pass the entire school day without learning more about the Chicken Man. After school, she was first to board the bus, eager to resume her conversation with her new friend. But each head popping into view was not his. Finally, the last two to board were Anthony and his chubby, freckled friend, Bo. These two plopped into the seat in front of hers.

Anthony, a tall black boy with lovely dimples whenever he smiled, glanced over his shoulder. "Victor's not coming," he said. "He's hanging with Billy."

Unable to consider such a contrary idea, Claire could only mumble, "Billy?" But then the grubby thought stuck, and she grabbed the back of Anthony's seat. "With Victor?" She was certain he was mistaken.

Anthony turned to Claire. He looked exotic to her, maybe as exotic as she looked to others. Dozens of tiny braids studded with colorful beads sprouted from his head, some dangling down a high forehead into the smiling eyes that generated so many schoolgirl crushes. Anthony propped his arm onto the back of the seat as Claire slid backward.

"They're gamers," he said.

"Gamers?"

Anthony shook his head and gave her a crooked smile, accentuating his dimples. "They're gamers like us." He pointed to Bo, the freckled boy sitting beside him who listened to music through a headset hidden beneath a tangle of rusty hair. "They play video games together."

"Oh," Claire said.

"Ask him about Flight Fever," he said, before turning away. "He'll tell you."

Claire sank into her seat, betrayed. Victor was friends with Billy? That monstrous boy? It didn't make sense.

She rolled her head against the window, staring blankly out its dirty pane. Jolted by a dreadful idea, she sat upright. *Unless... Victor isn't a nice person after all. What if he doesn't really like me?* Wide-eyed, she stared ahead, frozen in a panic of self-doubt.

4
Red-Belly and the Wolf Spider

Sammy met Claire at the bus for their walk, but she didn't want to go into the woods—not with the Chicken Man on the loose. Instead she headed to the store, smelling of new linoleum, with a disappointed dog trailing her steps. A few months earlier, Claire and her mother had moved from a tidy brick cottage at the edge of town into this old rambling house, with many small rooms, low ceilings, and crooked floors. It was said to be more than 150 years old, with a long, large room that had been a country store, which her mother planned to reopen. With the closest grocery store five miles away, in a modest shopping mall that included the bank, the post office, and the gas station, Louise's small grocery was sure to fill a large need in the rural community.

Their two-story wood frame home was evenly divided down the center, with the storeroom to the right and the living quarters to the left. This division was visible through a white wooden banister dividing the porch. Inside the house, a single oak swinging door separated the storeroom from their living room. Inside the storeroom, Sammy slumped onto the gold-speckled linoleum and, with a sigh of protest, dropped a heavy head onto his paw. Claire's mother stood inside a momentary shaft of sunlight, behind an antique mahogany case that served the prior storeowner. The bottom half of the case stored what the top displayed behind glass—all types of candy.

"Claire, tell me what you think," said her mother, pointing through the glass countertop. "Hard candies here and that entire area for chocolates and candy bars."

"Great, Mom," she said flatly.

"Okay. What's wrong?" Her mother was a woman of striking stature, almost six feet tall, with sandy hair falling thick and wavy to just below a strong, square jaw. Sammy raised an eye in her direction and sighed again. "Why aren't you two walking?"

"Just don't feel like it."

"Don't tell me then, but I'm busy, Claire. I've got a store to open in two weeks."

Claire stood with a sigh and headed behind the mahogany case to where a door led into the "summer" kitchen, a long, narrow room with an outside wall of windows. Before its walls contained wires for electricity or pipes for running water, this room had been where women canned the fruits and vegetables grown on the property. A black cast iron stove stood rooted, like an ancient artifact, in the room's center.

At the back door, Sammy flew past her legs into the brisk fall air, heading directly to the large pond, which lay behind and to the side of the house. As Sammy waded along the pond's edge to gulp water, Claire marched to the water's opposite side to sit beneath a huge Norwegian spruce to think hard thoughts. The idea that Victor would spend time with Billy was vexing. Other than Sammy and Victor, she had no friends, not even cousins, with whom to share her childhood. Having been home schooled until the sixth grade, she had had only her mother as confidante, friend, and teacher.

Sammy, full of playful energy, climbed out of the pond. He bolted and ran down the ivy-covered bank behind the pond that led to the creek. "Sammy!" Claire cried, but the dog disappeared into the woods. Her first thought was of the Chicken Man—a lunatic—who the night before stood where she now stood. And Sammy was loose. But what could she do?

He often ran off but always came back within the hour. She'd simply have to wait.

Upon the garden bench beneath the mighty spruce tree, she lay to gaze into its limbs. The scent of sap, sweet and heavy, soothed her. Up and up she wound her gaze like a white-breasted nuthatch climbs a tree. At each scaly limb, hung heavy with dark green needles, she paused to inspect for bird or bug. Within the sun-laced branches, she felt exalted, as if able to fly from a perch into the sky. Then a newcomer splintered the stillness. Claire slipped down the trunk with her gaze to a point directly overhead, where a red-bellied woodpecker gripped the trunk with his specialized toes: outside facing forward, inside facing backward. From over a shoulder, he looked down at her, crown and nape blazing red in a shaft of sun.

"Red-belly," she cooed. "You've come."

The black-and-white barred woodpecker hitched himself farther down the trunk.

Lifting gently onto elbows, she continued in a voice feather light, "I wish I knew why."

Claire stared at the woodpecker within a tight circle of the tree trunk. As she stared into the bird's red eyes, her peripheral vision began to fade and darken as if the world were vanishing. Oddly, she felt as if she, too, were fading, becoming less substantial. Then, with a single blink of her eyes, the world returned.

Leaning back on stiff tail feathers, the woodpecker surveyed the trunk where hunched a small but muscular wolf spider, eight eyes lit with sun. The woodpecker struck, and the wolf spider spun within the barbed tongue of its predator. Red-belly flew off as Claire raised herself upright while scanning her body. She stood and stomped each foot in turn, to solidify the form that seconds prior had begun to feel scanty. Confused and fretful, she ran for the safety of the house and her bedroom, where she might make sense of the experience.

Claire lay on her stomach in bed entering notes in a journal. Through the window, positioned on the wall where a headboard might otherwise be, she kept watch for Sammy who, after such outings, always refreshed himself in the pond. Though distracted, she penned her thoughts to paper, avoiding, for the moment, the most worrisome: her fading form and/or fading sight. To write of the episode would give it more reality and she mostly wanted to forget it. Instead, she focused on the question she asked herself everyday: Why do the birds I wear come to me? And today in her journal she wrote . . . *Did Red-Belly come for me or the wolf spider?*

Questions should have answers, but those crowding Claire's mind seemingly had none. How could a simple decal or screen-printed bird image attract its living subject? She had pondered this question for years, after first recognizing the connection. As a younger child, she had been certain it was magic, a charm cast upon her or the birds . . . but by whom? The answer then seemed obvious: her Irish grandmother and great-grandmother. Didn't these elders live in a fairy tale place called the Emerald Isle, where people believed in fairies? And weren't they the first to give her the gift of a screen-printed sweatshirt? Her Mamo and grandmother had come for the funeral of her father, killed in a trucking accident when she was three, and had taken them back to Ireland to stay an entire month. When they were leaving, her grandparents gave her a cotton sweatshirt with a colorful image of a red-tailed hawk, backlit by the sun, wings arched and raised above his shoulders. She remembered, even now, the thrill of first seeing it.

An Odd Bird

Closing her journal, she rolled off the bed to stare at herself in the dresser mirror. She saw an impostor, staring back with grayish-blue eyes. Over the years she had tried different colors of tinted lenses, but these were the most natural with her complexion and hair. As she prepared to remove the lenses from her amber eyes, the landline downstairs rang. Then her mother called up the stairs. "That's a neighbor, Mrs. Whiner. Sammy's at her house and she wants us to get him—now!"

Claire quickly joined her mother in the small coup wagon. The neighbor, an old widow, lived a quarter of a mile away, up a small hill leading out of the hollow wherein their house stood. They turned down a long dirt drive cutting through the woods, the air adrift with falling leaves. Around a sharp curve sat her rustic log home crowded with sheds and outbuildings. Behind and below the house sat a gray, weathered barn. Claire could hear Sammy and another dog barking as she and her mother circled the house, pulling up to the back. Two gray cats perched on a porch railing jumped and scurried away. A sour-faced woman with eyes pinched to the bridge of her hooked nose pushed through the kitchen door.

"I won't have that stray coming here to bark at my birds," she said angrily, throwing a hand toward a pigeon loft. "People round here shoot strays!"

"Where is he?" Claire asked, jumping out of the car, concerned only with her dog's rescue. She didn't wait for an answer but followed the sound of his urgent barks. She found Sammy tied to the bumper of a rusting truck set atop concrete blocks right inside the woods on the other side of the house. She could hear the other dog barking but couldn't see where he was.

5
Save the Beagle

Saturday morning, with gold and red leaves whipping in the wind, Claire jumped on her mountain bike and pedaled hard up the road. She was heading to see Victor, who held answers to her crop of itchy, prickly questions about Billy and the Chicken Man. These had irritated her throughout the evening and into the night. Now her discomfort was extreme.

At the hill's crest, the road fell away, and through the air she flew for an instant until tires met asphalt. Out in front, above the road, a hawk appeared, swooping earthward toward her. Its outstretched wings filled the sky above her upward-looking face. Its white breast bore a cinnamon cross. It was Jerry and Becky's hawk from the woodland! Showing flashes of ruddy tail, she banked and was gone. The two had passed—one above, the other below—only feet away. Held by the downhill speed of her bike, Claire couldn't look back but finished the hill, with outstretched arms, like wings, slicing through the air.

Fresh air and exertion cleansed Claire of her prior frustrations. She pulled up to Victor's house, a one-story frame with a patch of yard, jumped off her bike, and knocked rapidly on the door. Hair tousled, Victor answered, wearing sweatpants and a T-shirt. "Hey," he said drowsily.

"Victor, you won't believe it—a red-tailed hawk just zoomed me on the road!" But her news had no effect. He glanced away into the house and narrowed the door opening. Looking out, face half hidden, he said, "What do you want?"

Embarrassed, she said, "Did I wake you?" This was her

first (and maybe last) visit to Victor's home.

"I've been up half the night." He looked away, back into the house.

She dropped her eyes. "I couldn't wait to hear about the Chicken Man."

The door swung suddenly open and a thin woman with dyed blond hair and a worry-worn face filled the frame. "When I'm not here, he's not allowed friends in," she said emphatically, stepping back to admit the unannounced guest. "And he's allowed out only with prior permission. I can't focus at work worrying where in the world he might be." Claire nodded obediently, not sure what next to do. "Well, come in, come in," the woman demanded. "I'm getting ready to leave, so you won't have much time."

Claire stepped into the cramped living room as Victor plopped onto a worn couch, from where he watched his mother descend steps into the finished basement. "I'll meet you at your house in about an hour."

"Your mother will give her permission?" Claire asked dutifully, but Victor dismissed the question with a wave of hand and toss of head, as if what his mother wanted didn't matter.

Claire waited for Victor outside, at the pond with Sammy. Since racing home, she had helped her mother arrange shelving aisles in the storeroom and had made cucumber, tomato, and mayonnaise sandwiches. Waiting for his arrival was not easy with a shaggy sheepdog eager to go on a walk. Sammy bounded about her, saying, "Come on! Let's go, let's go—the woodland calls!" Yet she ignored him, even distracted him with a biscuit, holding it up but then hiding it away. Still, Sammy forgave her when the stranger arrived.

After a rollicking introduction, the three raced over the narrow macadam road and into the high, now drying, pasture grasses. Sammy led the way over mowed paths into the woodland anchored by a massive white oak. On its mighty raised roots, they sat as Sammy bounded down to the creek to plunge into his favorite water hole, aglitter with afternoon sun.

"Anthony told me that you're a 'gamer.'" Claire handed him a sandwich loosely wrapped in wax paper.

"I love tomato sandwiches," he said, taking a big bite. "Yeah, I'm on the computer all the time." He wiped mayonnaise from his lips. "That's why I was up half the night."

Claire studied her lunch, still unwrapped. "He said you play videos with Billy."

Victor lowered his sandwich. "I've told him not to call you names, Claire." He sought her downcast eyes. "He's just jealous because you're my friend. We're on a mission to Mars," he said, taking another bite, speaking as he chewed. "Billy's actually super smart, even if he acts like a dolt."

From the creek, Sammy came lunging toward them, one hundred pounds of muscle and sopping creek-cold fur. "He's going to shake!" cried Claire, scrambling to her feet, stumbling to dodge the delirious dog who would certainly douse them. As he did, they merrily shrieked against the pelting spray. Giggling, the friends dashed toward a circle of sun with Sammy chasing after, his wooly coat still dripping water. To divert him, Claire threw the dog biscuit and then settled upon the warmth of a large flat stone. From a deep jacket pocket, she retrieved the somewhat smashed sandwich and offered Victor half. They were both happy to start again with another topic, the Chicken Man.

Victor remained unconvinced that any encounter with the Chicken Man could be innocent and told her of his history. He had never married but worked on his father's dairy farm until his parents died, when he himself was a middle-aged man. The Chicken Man's older brother inherited the farm and let him stay on, though everyone knew he was good for nothing but tending the chickens and baking pies. Otherwise, he spent time in the woods, like some crazy mountain man. But when the Chicken Man's brother died a few years back, his sister-in-law sold the farm.

Claire was enthralled by Victor's story. Never before had he spoken so much or with such enthusiasm. And she loved to listen to the pitch of his voice, rising and falling in a musical way. More melodic than a simple accent, his intonations were lyrical, almost as sweet to her ear as birdsong. "The Chicken Man had to move into town, but he hated it and never bathed or left the town house. When the landlord found he was keeping chickens in a bedroom, they took them away and he really went crazy."

"But I saw him with Becky," Claire protested, "a Rhode Island Red."

"Then he must've hid one or else got another." Victor told her how the Chicken Man would save junk mail to throw at the mail carrier, how on Halloween he had tied a kid to his front porch post, and most frightening—how he was now stealing dogs. "Who knows what he does with those poor dogs," Victor said with a moan.

"I saw him," Claire sputtered, "the Chicken Man, the other night at our pond. He had a beagle!"

"He knows where you live?" Victor was horrified.

"I don't know! But I saw him with a beagle. It was midnight."

"Poor beagle," Victor wailed. "What should we do?"

"We have to save him!" cried Claire, jumping up.

☙ Save the Beagle ☙

Victor too hopped up. "But I can't today," he said apologetically, sensitive to her disappointment. "Will do it tomorrow, for sure."

6
Chasing the Chicken Man

Sammy watched woefully from the living room bay window as Claire and Victor crossed the road and headed through the pasture. He had been left behind because a sheepdog couldn't be trusted on a spy mission. Under the late afternoon sun, they bounded down to the creek, where well-placed rocks provided a stepping bridge. On the other side, they climbed a steep hill through towering hemlock. They moved quickly along a well-traveled deer path, softly padded by hemlock needles, scenting the crisp air. Soon Claire pointed to a hillside thick with young hemlocks. "We go down here. There's a ledge of sort. That's where I saw the Chicken Man sitting under a hemlock." A snapping twig drew their attention. Far below, something reddish brown fluttered from a tree to the ground.

"A chicken," Victor said, somewhat confused.

"Becky!" Claire gasped. And with panic-filled voices, both cried, "the Chicken Man!"

"Hurry!" Claire yelled. And the two wildly ran opposite the hillside, stumbling over fallen limbs, bursting through brittle tree branches, and lunging toward a fallen hemlock. They dove over its massive trunk and rolled onto the ground. Claire peered through a hole in the decaying trunk.

"Do you see him yet?" Victor whispered.

"Not yet."

"What about Becky?"

"Wait!" hissed Claire. "I see his head."

Both tucked their heads deep to the ground. Becky cackled and fluttered in their direction, landing in crunchy leaves. She scratched and pecked at the ground only feet from their heads.

"Becky Bonnet, get your pecking head over here," came a gruff voice from a safer distance, and the chicken scampered away, obedient as a dog. The terrified pair warily lifted their faces above the decaying tree. The Chicken Man was quickly moving away, with Becky chasing after. They waited until he was far ahead to trail him but found it difficult to keep up. The old man followed a network of deer paths and lumber roads that eventually pushed into territory unknown by Claire. Luckily, he followed a property line—a straight march of tree trunks, each with a single blaze of white paint—which would lead them home again.

In the fading day, under nearly naked trees, they pursued the Chicken Man through a field of mountain laurel. Uneasy in the open, they leaped through this laurel like deer through a thicket while the Chicken Man pushed ahead through a thick stand of white pine trees, disappearing from sight. Afraid to lose him, Claire and Victor thrust through the branches, never expecting what lay beyond: a massive outcrop of stone, flat like a tabletop. The Chicken Man headed to its ledge and sat on a boulder, staring into the expanse of deepening sky.

The two froze—a backward glance by the lunatic would reveal them. Just then Becky squawked in distress. The Chicken Man turned in their direction, a startled look upon his face. Jumping up, he charged toward them across the outcrop. Claire clamped her eyes shut, and Victor sagged in the knees as the bearded man bore down, pushing between them toward his chicken fluttering on a tree branch above a barking dog.

"Sammy!" Claire shrieked.

The sheepdog dashed to her, bathing Claire with his tongue. "How did you find us?" she cried, kneeling to embrace her protector. But standing over them now was the Chicken

Man, and Sammy lowered his head in submission.

"Get up!" he ordered, glowering at Claire. "Why are you two stalking me?"

She could utter but two words. "The beagle."

"What beagle?" He demanded, his grizzly face inches from hers.

"You—you—kidnapped it!" Victor squeaked.

Baffled, the old man scoured his scalp as if to get blood to his brain. "Would either of you say something that makes sense?!"

No one noticed, not even Sammy, that Becky was pecking her way onto the rock outcrop. But from a high distance, a red-tailed hawk did note the plump red bird preening herself and began a diving descent.

Claire was the first to see and bellowed, "Hawk!"

The old man turned in horror, and all three watched the fierce raptor descending from the sky, extending its cruel talons, ready for the grab. But Sammy appeared, lunging as if to snatch the hawk from the air. A powerful whoosh of wings and the majestic marauder lifted skyward, without her prey.

Becky scurried to Jerry, who lifted her to his shoulder, and Claire ran to Sammy, who howled in protest of the retreating hawk. When Claire and Victor looked again toward the old man, they saw his face buried against Becky's soft feathers. Awkwardly looking away, they sneaked peeks at one another while Jerry drew a handkerchief from the pocket of his overalls to blow his nose. After a bit, he looked out into the sky. "See?" He pointed to a soaring speck. "Big Red's still out there."

Now all were crossing the outcrop, eyes and minds fixed on the sky. "Where?" Victor asked.

"There! See her circling? She's riding an updraft of warm air." Claire spotted the raptor without effort and slipped the binoculars from her neck to give to Victor.

"The score's two to nothing, and Becky wins again," Jerry said, stroking Becky's breast as he lowered to sit upon the boulder. Both children squatted where they stood, scooting to dangle their legs over the outcrop's ledge. Sammy sat between them. Everyone gazed into the expanse of unlimited sky and rolling mountains, ablaze with fall color. The hawk could still be seen soaring in the deepening heavens of her world.

"Becky isn't the only chicken 'round here," Jerry continued, "and those who raise 'em don't like Big Red. But some have a high opinion of her." He took a long drink from a canteen slung over one shoulder. "Half dozen or more years back, this young mother went into the woods with her little daughter for a picnic. Seems it was a warm spring day, and the two napped a bit. But when the mother woke up, the daughter was gone."

"That was me!" cried Claire, scuttling backward from the edge, Sammy pouncing about her. She quickly stood. "My mother told me the story—that was me!"

Jerry stared at her, seemingly amazed

"What?" said Victor, pulling up his legs to scoot from the edge and then to stand. "What?" He looked expectantly from one to the other.

Still holding his chicken, Jerry shifted to address Victor. "That mother frantically searched for her little girl before going for help. While Kelly called the police, a man in the store went with her to the picnic blanket to scout the area, with no luck. But then he spotted a hawk flying in a tight circle around the crown of a large oak. It called again and again and again—with that raspy scream—like it was trying to get someone's attention. Well, this man led the mother toward that tree, and there, lying against the trunk, was the little girl, sleeping."

"It sounds like a fairy tale." Victor looked in wonder at Claire, now lost in thought.

She stood, head bowed, staring at the image imprinted on her shirt of a red-tailed hawk. In that moment, she might have risked telling Victor about her secret relationship with birds, but not with Jerry present. She never told anyone, not even her mother. She feared that doing so might break the spell, if it were a spell that drew them to her. Yet Claire hardly believed in this childhood theory anymore. Even so, there had to be some reason. If only she could share the mystery with a friend who could help her solve it. At the least, she might share a clue.

"Want to hear something else, something pretty strange?" she said, looking first to Victor and then Jerry. "On that day when Big Red found me, I was wearing my first ever T-shirt with a silk screen image of a bird—a red-tailed hawk. And look"—she glanced down at her shirt—"I'm wearing a hawk again, today."

"Now, that is a strange coincidence," said Jerry. He paused to look at the white-haired girl anew before slapping a thigh. "Well, it's getting late," he said, heaving upward, Becky clutched firmly in his arm. "You had better get going."

Sammy led the way off the rock outcrop, followed by Claire, Victor, and Jerry. When all were on the soft ground, Claire asked, "But what about that beagle? I did see you with one, at midnight, by our pond."

Jerry chuckled, speaking softly to Becky roosting comfortably on his shoulder. "I've been found out, huh girl?" Turning to Claire, he said, "I walk that beagle every full moon. That's why I call him Moon Doggy. His real name is Schooner." He explained that Moon Doggy had belonged to his best friend, now dead a year. "Mike and I would come out with Schooner to this overlook every day. After Mike died, I asked his widow—your neighbor, Helen Whiner—if I could have the beagle, but she said no out of spite. She never liked me, you see. So I took matters into my own hands. Once a month we go walking in the moonlight till dawn."

"Does the widow know?" Claire asked.

"Of course not!" he barked so belligerently that she jumped. "Didn't you hear what I said? She don't like me!"

Claire and Victor swapped surprised looks. Clearly, they did not yet know with whom they dealt. Even so, they couldn't help admiring the Chicken Man, who didn't kidnap dogs but rescued them, in the moonlight, at midnight, and without permission. The joy of it made them somewhat giddy.

"Can we go with you and Moon Doggy next time?" Victor asked earnestly.

"No! Now get home, the both of you."

7
A Horrible Discovery

At dinner that evening, Louise suggested that they bake a pie for the widow Whiner as a peace offering for Sammy's trespass of two days prior. Claire was quick to agree, since she could then investigate the widow's pigeons. On Monday, after school, she trotted up the road with pie in hand, thinking about Victor, who hadn't gone to school that day. Against the cold and wind, she wore several layers beneath her white sweatshirt sporting the image of a wild turkey. The sky was tight with high gray clouds rippling like sand. Through it flew a long, snaking band of blackbirds.

The widow was sweeping her back porch as Claire swooped in. "Hello, Mrs. Whiner! We baked you a pie."

The widow held the broom beside her like a staff. "Tell me it ain't apple 'cause that's my least favorite."

"It's French apple," Claire said hopefully, stepping up to the porch and holding the pie out for inspection.

"It'll do. Come in, then." A tabby cat dodged between the widow's legs and under her brown flannel skirt as she opened the door to the kitchen. "Darn those cats!"

Claire put the pie onto a large but cluttered kitchen table, big enough to seat a dozen people, though the widow lived alone. Piles of mail and magazines sprawled across the ripped plastic tablecloth. Bags, boxes, and cans of cat food crowded the other end.

"This pie is to say 'thank you' for calling us to get Sammy."

"Yeah, I know what the pie's for, young lady," said the widow, squinting at Claire. She pulled a frayed red sweater across her thin chest. "You look like a boy with that short hair; stop cutting it off!"

Claire didn't know what to say. She stroked the short, soft waves covering her scalp and thought of Jerry, also short-tempered. Were all old people so cranky? Possessed of a sudden idea, she said, "You know Jerry, right?"

"And who wants to know?"

Perplexed, she said, "I do."

Helen Whiner grunted her irritation. "It's an expression, Miss Smarty-Pants." Digging a bobby pin from an apron pocket, the widow anchored a loose wisp of gray hair to her scalp, studded with many such pins. "Whether I know that bum is none of your business."

Claire traced her finger over a tear in the plastic tablecloth. "It's just that Jerry likes that beagle—"

"So Jerry, the fabulous pie maker, put you up to this!" Helen's stingy eyes flared with emotion.

"My mom made that pie!" Claire cried so righteously that the old woman modified her indignation.

"Well, don't count on buttering me up with pie," she grumbled.

Claire was eager to change the subject. "Are those homing pigeons?" She pressed far over the sink to better see the loft through the kitchen window.

"Don't be silly, girl. What else would they be?"

"Who's that man?" she next asked, pointing to someone walking toward the loft. The widow didn't answer but scurried to the kitchen door.

"Clyde!" she yelled, the screen door slamming behind her. "Are you going to clean that loft today or what?"

The man, who wore navy overalls crusty with dried pigeon droppings, stepped into the loft, quickly shutting the door.

Helen charged back into the kitchen. "I nearly have to beg that lazy nephew of mine to tend to those pigeons. And I pay him good money, too!"

"Do you think he'd let me help?"

"If you don't mind pigeon poop, be my guest," she said, marching into the next room. Claire dove toward the door just as it opened from the outside—and into the room stepped Billy.

"Bird Girl!" he cried in surprise.

Claire froze as one encountering a snake. She stepped slowly backward.

"Billy, is that you?" barked the widow, charging back into the kitchen. "Get that hair out of your eyes, or I'll pin it back myself!" She dug into her apron and lunged for Billy, who darted out the screen door. He spilled down the steps and ran toward some outbuildings. "Don't think I can't find you, Billy!" she called and then grabbed Claire by the wrist, pulling her onto the porch. "Chase after him, girl. Don't give 'im a chance to hide."

"Huh?"

"Hurry! He's givin' you the slip!"

Claire tumbled down the steps, certain of nothing but the wild look in Helen's eyes. She trotted after Billy, who fled behind a long, narrow shed. Moon Doggy barked frantically from the other side of the barn. Claire had no interest in finding Billy, but she did want to see the lonely beagle.

She circled around the barn, stopping just long enough to peek through one of its missing boards. Inside, half a dozen cats were lounging on hay bales, protected from the fierce gusting wind. When the sun slipped from behind a dark cloud, the gray walls blazed with stripes of light. On seeing Claire turn the barn corner, the beagle leaped into the air and then darted back and forth to the length of his short chain. He was

A Horrible Discovery

nearly too wild to approach, but Claire dropped to her knees, pulling from her pocket two biscuit bones.

"Look what I brought you, Moon Doggy," she said to the desperate dog, who grabbed a bone, dropped it, and then raced in a tight circle.

"Calm down, Moon Doggy. Let me pet you."

"Stop calling him Moon Doggy!" barked Billy from behind. He walked to the side and whistled, but the beagle ignored him. "No one's allowed to pet him!"

"Says who?"

"Says me!"

"I'll pet him whenever I want!"

Like an angry bull, Billy began to snort, his face flushing red. Then an idea flashed in his solitary eye as clearly as a wink. His pressed lips slid into a smile. "Hey, do you want to see a hawk?"

Claire snapped her face skyward to a patch of blue among the treetops. "Where?"

"Not there," he said, moving away. "Follow me." But Claire didn't follow, and he had to turn back. "I'm telling you, there's a hawk perched on this one tree branch—"

"Since when do you watch birds?" she asked. He was baiting her. But why?

"Hawks aren't 'birds,'" he said snidely. "They're raptors."

She gave the straining, whining beagle one last caress and stood to leave. "I won't go anywhere with you!"

He ignored her declaration. "I think it's a red-shouldered hawk; I'm not sure." He pointed toward the pasture. "It's just there!"

Claire could not disregard a hawk sighting, especially not of a red-shouldered hawk. She followed him, despite misgivings, to a long metal utility shed beside the barn. "I've got to grab binoculars," he said, opening its steel door. He clicked on a row of fluorescent lights as she stood at the threshold. A wide metalwork table filled the floor space and perched on its edge was a hawk—eyes wide in alarm and wings unfolding for flight. Claire ducked, eyes shut against the swoop of talons to come... But the air was still. Then she heard a wicked, crooning laugh.

"It's stuffed, stupid!"

Claire peered from under her forearm. "Oh, no!" she cried, running from the door.

"My father shot and stuffed it," Billy called, but Claire thought only to hide from this horrible scene and from him. She darted toward the barn, hoping to slip through its partly opened door before he could turn the corner. Inside she scaled a ladder to a hayloft and hid in a corner behind several bales of hay, her nostrils filling with its scent. All the cats had scattered but one, a calico who sat atop three bales and looking down at her. Through a crack in the barn wall, Claire could see Moon Doggy below, his howls muffled by the sound of her own pounding heart.

Having lost Claire's trail, Billy backtracked to the doghouse. "Shut up, you stupid dog!"

Claire clambered to her feet, straining to see through the wallboard cracks of the barn. Below her, Moon Doggy cowered beneath the frustrated boy kicking up dirt at him. "No!" she shouted angrily from above. "You stop it!"

Billy flew toward the barn, allowing Claire no time to descend from the loft as he broke through the door below. "I'll tell your aunt!" she screamed down at him.

"Who cares? She's crazy!" he yelled, heading straight for the ladder. With each rung he climbed, Claire took one step backward until Billy's head rose above the loft floor.

A Horrible Discovery

"It's illegal to shoot red-tails!" she shouted, angry but scared, standing behind a tall tier of hay bales.

"Who cares?" he said, scaling the remaining rungs. "My dad does whatever he wants." He now stood on the loft floor. "And he's going to get an even bigger and better hawk."

An impulse seized Claire to rush and push Billy off the loft, the urge so strong it scared her. Instead she shoved the top hay bale with the might of her fury and screamed, "I'll tell the game commission!"

Billy stopped. Watching her warily with his exposed eye, he combed the hair covering the right eye with his fingers. "Better not," he said finally. "Or I'll make things bad for you with Victor."

A shrill cry rang through the air—"Bill-eeeee"—so piercing that even Moon Doggy stopped barking. Helen stood right outside the barn. Billy spun around to quickly descend the ladder, but before disappearing beneath the loft floor, he gave one final warning. "And don't even think about messing with my dog. I'll know if you do."

On her way home, Claire blazed a new path through the woods, snapping twigs with a vengeance. Billy was worse than she had imagined. How could Victor possibly be his friend? Skidding downward over slippery leaves, she dropped onto a rolling hillside ledge just as a wild turkey scurried toward her.

"Tuk-tuk, tuk-tuk!" the bird cried in alarm, diving off the ledge to dodge the girl. Feathers brushed her face as the turkey glided toward an open branch.

"Tuk-tuk, tuk-tuk, tuk-tuk, tuk-tuk," a chorus of alarm rose around her as many startled birds, a least a dozen, crashed through the underbrush with hard-beating wings. Claire whirled about, pulled by sound, groping for sight of the escaping birds. Some hopped from branch to branch, others

❧ *An Odd Bird* ❧

skimmed the sky above the tree line. Dark shadows against a dusky-gray sky. Though the flock disappeared too soon, Claire held the thrill in her blood.

8
Moon Woman

Claire had wanted to tell her mother about the horrible encounter with Billy, that his father had killed and stuffed a red-tailed hawk, that Billy had threatened her in the barn. But her mother would report it to the authorities, and Billy would get back at her. She couldn't risk it.

Victor, however, deserved to know, and she had to tell him. Learning the truth would disturb him because he loved and respected animals. The Cochiti believed that animals—cougar, bear, wolf, badger, mole, eagle—were spirit helpers to humans. And his people especially revered eagles, who were powerful in body and spirit. As Victor had explained, possessing an eagle feather gave its bearer protection from evil as well as higher levels of consciousness.

On Tuesday morning Claire boarded the school bus heavy with resolve. She would tell Victor everything, including that Billy had threatened her in the widow's barn. Would such news outrage her new friend? Would it send him charging off the bus in search of that wicked, donkey-faced boy? She wanted Victor to shove Billy and knock that stupid patch of hair from over his right eye. But Victor boarded the bus wearing a surly expression and sat on the seat's edge, with his back to her.

"What's wrong?" she asked, crestfallen.

"I was grounded two weeks because of you."

Instantly she understood. Victor's mother had learned that he left the house without permission on Sunday while she was at work. "I didn't make you go," she said, pleading over his shoulder, but he sprang from the seat to sit across the aisle. She stared at him, speechless, unsure what to say or do. Never before had he behaved so rudely! Over the bench seat she slid toward the aisle, reaching for his shoulder when Anthony, sitting in the seat ahead, turned to speak to him.

"You guys out Monday with a 'fever'"? he said, grinning.

Victor noticeably brightened. "You bet. Most of the day and then again into the night."

Claire gaped at Victor's sudden improvement of mood.

"You level-up?"

"What do you think?"

Anthony chuckled. "I think you're a maniac," he said and turned away.

Confused and resentful, Claire slid on the bench seat away from the aisle and toward the window. She crossed her chest with folded arms, determined not to look at or talk to Victor for the duration of the trip. Churning inside, she stared through the window at the gray day. How could he treat her so badly after their adventure chasing the Chicken Man? After Jerry declared Big Red to be the hawk of her childhood story? And how incredible for that same hawk to find her again, not once but three times—in the woods with Sammy, above her on the road, and at the outcrop. These encounters were but part of a larger mystery, one she was desperate to solve. Victor could help her; she knew it. Yet he sat ignoring her across the aisle.

Her dark mood deepened when sighting Billy, standing curbside in front of the school. Each window glided by Billy's upturned face as Victor hopped from his seat. Claire pulled down the windowpane to stare at her foe, whose solitary eye bore into her own, yet she would not look away, not until Victor spilled onto the sidewalk. Then she watched as Victor and Billy walked off together.

After school, Claire sat in the backseat of the bus, a blatant trespass against the rosy-cheeked twin brothers who daily occupied it. The third-graders stood in the aisle gawking, unsure what to do until she offered each a candy bar to sit in another seat. Her plan was to ignore Victor as he had earlier ignored her, but he found her slouched in the backseat.

"You forgive me, right?" He plopped cheerfully down beside her. "I was in a mood," he said, glancing around. Claire, however, did not want to forgive so easily. He had not only hurt her feelings but also denied her the opportunity to tell what weighted so heavily on her heart. She sat upright but stared out the window. Victor twisted toward her. "I'm sorry. It isn't your fault that I got grounded. I lashed out."

"You were nice enough to Anthony," she reminded him.

"He was asking about my Mars Mission."

"It's just a game!"

"No," he said too loudly, "it's training!" Regretting this tone, he continued in an explanatory way. "NASA developed Flight Fever for kids interested in space travel. The game even connects to real-time NASA missions. Billy and I have been training since second grade to become crew members for this virtual trip to Mars."

The revelation stunned her. Billy's claim to Victor clearly exceeded hers. They were childhood friends united in a space adventure. "Oh," she said timidly. She had imagined that he shared her passions for animals and the Earth.

"Can I give you a Cochiti name?" he asked in a sudden whisper, tucking his head down. "A name that only I can call you?"

Claire could see that he felt guilty and was trying to please her, and the tactic worked. She looked to him expectantly, lowering her face toward his. "You mean like Soaring Eagle?"

"Yes, something like that, but I was thinking . . ." He had, in fact, given the idea much thought. "Tahwach K'uyaw."

The exotic words made her feel the same. "What does it mean?"

"Moon Woman."

Her hopeful expression faded. "Because of my hair and skin?"

"Don't be silly." He grinned. "Because you're as radiant as the moon."

Radiant. The word revived her like rain on a dry plant. She sat bolt upright, but another concern surfaced. "Woman—not girl?"

He, too, sat upright. "Won't you be twelve this summer?"

"Yes . . . but can you say it again?"

"Tahwach K'uyaw . . . Moon Woman."

Claire whispered it tentatively. Accepting a new name was no insignificant thing. Though awkward in her mouth, the words sounded lyrical. "I love it!" she said finally. "Can I tell my mother?"

"No! It's just between us. Okay?"

"Yes!" she cried, thrilled to share this secret with Victor. "What's your Cochiti name?"

"I won't tell you just yet," he said, tilting his head playfully.

9
Midnight Rescue

That night, a school night, the waning moon climbed higher into the black night sky. From her bedroom window, Claire watched its progress, thinking of her new native name—Moon Woman—and Victor. She smiled with the thought. Even so, beneath this pleasure she still felt resentment because Victor was an ally of her enemy.

She waited for the midnight hour, when she would crawl onto the tin roof and climb down the maple tree. She was following Jerry's example: if he could walk the beagle in the moonlight, so could she. Billy couldn't tell her what to do. She also wanted to get back at Victor for Billy's terrible misdeeds, which weighed heavily on her because she couldn't tell him, her only friend. Claire thought with satisfaction that Victor was right to call her Moon Woman. Under the moon this night she would walk the beagle without him.

She closed the bedroom door to Sammy, who slept in the hall with legs and paws propped against the wall. Any noise might alert him, and the scraping sound of the window sliding up its track made her cringe. From a warm bed, centered beneath this window, she crawled into the cold night air and onto the wet, slippery tin roof. In the light from her bedroom window, two strong limbs of the maple tree reached out to her.

At the base of the tree, she checked her gear, deciding to return home when the moon dipped into the west. Claire wasn't afraid of the dark, since she spent long nights stargazing with her mother, who was happiest under a moonless night sky studded, splattered, and sprayed with stars—red, yellow, and blue stars. But Claire liked the silver sheen of the world under a full moon and the way her mother's hair glowed silver in the moonlight.

She climbed the road leading uphill and away from her home, which sat in a hollow on Kelly Store Road. At the crest of the hill, the macadam turned sharply left, where ramshackle houses sat huddled together, their smoking chimneys filling the air with the smell of wood fires. But Claire followed a dirt drive to the right, cutting into the woods toward the widow's home.

Within the black branches of naked trees, the moon slid through the sky; lattices of shadow lay on the twisting lane. Scanning the open branches with her naked golden eyes, Claire's night vision grew sharper. The night had no need for the timid, blue-tinted eyes she showed to the day.

Though the cold night air made white vapor of her breath, she felt overly warm and stopped to shed her outermost sweatshirt, with the image of a barred owl perched on a dead tree limb against a full moon. She tied it about her waist. Jogging headlong around the last bend in the lane, she sprinted across a packed dirt lot in front of the widow's house and followed it to the back. From the top of a sloping wooded hill, she looked down to the barn, over which hung the bright moon. The beagle lay sleeping on the other side, chained to his doghouse. A ribbon of moonlight lit the way over shallow steps graded into the wooded hillside. With light, swift steps she glided toward the barn and was soon tiptoeing up to the doghouse.

When he saw Claire, Moon Doggy spun excitedly in tight circles, making it difficult to grab his collar. When he was finally hooked to a leash secured about her waist, he pulled her forward, like a horse pulling a plow, back up the hillside. At the top, they rushed toward the loft, carried on an irresistible current of pigeon scent. A ragged black cloud hid the moon as they plunged into woods behind the loft. And then she was pitching downward, onto her hands.

Grunting in pain, she pushed up from the ground, feeling the pull of the dog's leash toward the object beside her. In the absence of moonlight, it appeared as a large rectangular box centered in a bald circle of packed dirt. Some piece of junk, Claire thought, sitting now to rub the shin of her injured leg. Yet the beagle's enthusiasm perplexed her. With tail wildly wagging, he stepped toward it and back again, as if dancing.

Free of its black shroud, the moon flooded the scene in pale, cool light. Reaching for the flashlight, Claire felt something lurch within the rectangular box. Falling backward, she scuttled away on hands and feet, yanking the dog with her. Whining, the beagle strained against the leash, insistent as a spoiled child. But Claire pushed farther back, heels digging the dirt, bottom scraping the ground, her progress stopped, finally, by a young birch tree.

Intently Claire watched for more movement within the box. Then she hurriedly unhooked the beagle from her waist, wrapping and knotting his leash around the birch tree's slender trunk before scooping the flashlight from the ground. With a deep breath, she shed light onto the mystery. What met her eyes was a wood-framed box with welded metal wire panels—a cage.

"What?" Claire said, approaching more closely, bending toward it on one knee. "What is this?"

Crouching within this cage, with splayed wings and lowered head, was a hawk. The cruelty of it made her gasp. For seconds she stared, immobilized. With a pounding heart, she inspected the trapdoor, looking for a way to release its victim, whose one talon had been snagged by the door's trip wire.

"It's okay," she said as much to herself as to the hawk, the light shining into one of its glaring brown eyes. And then she saw it—the crimson cross. The hawk was Big Red.

Claire became suddenly fearless. Her only thought was to help Big Red, the hawk who three times in three days had encountered her. Some mystery bound them in spirit. The raptor's razor-sharp beak and talons mattered not. With her father's Swiss Army knife, she first fished for the vertical trip wire in which the hawk's talon was tangled. Pulling at this wire with the hook of the can opener tool, she raised it through the top grating and then sliced it with the knife. The hawk's leg fell free to the cage bottom, its claw still entangled with a monofilament line. Grabbing the sweatshirt about her waist, Claire wrapped her right hand and forearm within the fabric and opened the trapdoor with her left. Plunging her arm into the cage, she urged to the hawk, "Get on, get on. I can lift you out. Just get on."

Big Red stared into Claire's eyes. Their locking gaze formed a bridge and the hawk lunged upward to first fall across her arm and then to sink the talons of her free claw into the soft fabric for support. Claire slowly pulled her arm outward as Big Red flared her folded wings for balance, one limp leg trailing behind. Once clear of the trapdoor, Big Red raised her entwined leg, propping it upon the perch of Claire's arm.

"I have to untangle your claw," she said to the hawk, who remained complacent on her perch. If Moon Doggy barked, Claire didn't hear, caught up entirely in her effort to unwind the monofilament line from the hawk's leg and claw. And when done, with not a second of delay, she thrust up her arm as the hawk unfolded miraculous wings, pulling upward into the air. Claire sank to the ground under the wind of the hawk's wings. Big Red was airborne and free.

10
Call of the Barred Owl

For some moments, Claire lay back flat against the ground, motionless, existing in some non-physical place among the stars. Almost imperceptibly at first, the sound of a persistent whining came to her ears. It grew in volume only as her attention moved toward it from the quiet heavens. Suddenly loud and frantic, the sound exploded on her eardrums and she jolted upright. The beagle, bound tightly against the tree, was crying in distress. Climbing to her feet, she unhooked him as he plunged toward the cage.

"She's gone now," Claire said. "I freed her." But the beagle persisted in his attention to the rectangular frame.

"Moon Doggy, you have to go home now," she said, approaching to hook him to the leash. But the beagle dodged her, running to the other side of the cage. That's when she noticed a white clump shining in the moonlight. What was it? A rag? Yet the flashlight showed something else: a dead pigeon. She shuddered with this new horror, wanting only to leave yet knowing she couldn't. In a yellow ring of light, she saw the pigeon's one leg tethered to the back-cage wall. In an instant she understood. The innocent bird had been used as live bait for the hawk. Claire had no doubt that this was the diabolical handiwork of Billy's father, the man who had already killed and stuffed another red-tail.

Through the wire grating, she cut the pigeon's tether and then jostled the cage to dislodge the bird, which rolled nearer to the trapdoor. Scooting onto her stomach, she reached in to clutch it, stiff and cold, its downy feathers still soft to the touch.

Into the pouch of her sweatshirt she stuffed the lifeless bird and kicked the cage in outrage. Startled, the beagle skidded away, heading toward the ridge above the creek.

"Moon Doggy—don't!" she called, chasing after him, but he instantly dove down the ridge side, heading for the creek below. The moonlight lay serenely over the ridge like a thin film of snow. Below her the beagle plunged into a deep, sparkling water hole. He paddled in tight circles, his head skimming the surface like a beaver.

"Moon Doggy!" Claire called. "Come with me!"

Pulling himself from the water, the dog shook his coat, looked upward toward her, and then trotted downstream.

"No!" she called, descending the hillside, skidding on her heels, slipping on her bottom, and grabbing at saplings to slow her speed. These antics interested the beagle enough to stop and watch, but as she stood creekside to brush her scraped and burning palms, he pushed ahead.

Claire looked skyward for the moon, her bright companion, just as a dark serpentine cloud swallowed it whole. And already Moon Doggy was beyond reach of the flashlight. Should she chase him?

An answer came immediately: Hoooo!

Loud as a trumpet and lyrical as a flute, the barred owl's call echoed in the night.

Hoo-hoo-hoo-hoaaa!

The call was so near, so irresistible, seemingly just beyond the flashlight's reach. Soon she was chasing behind its tunnel of yellow light.

"Wait for me; wait for me," she pleaded to the beagle, plunging through the night with a rapid-fire heart. From the blackness beyond, decaying tree stumps rushed to block her, branches to grab her, slippery rocks to trip her—but she dodged each threat. Suddenly she was plowing into the dog, his nose glued to the ground by some scent. Yet with a yelp, he scampered away from the creek, running deep into the woods.

The moon reappeared, again flooding the woods with light. Fearless, she decided to chase him, though it meant leaving the creek, her pathway home. Frozen dew sparkled like diamond dust over the ground. Again, she stopped to listen for the low roar of the creek but heard instead a dog's bark. Atop a low ridge, Moon Doggy skirted a tree and then strained against its trunk for scent of a porcupine. Claire ran toward the tree, but the dog dodged her yet again.

Girl and beagle followed the ridgetop, where the wind began to howl. All suddenly went dark. She couldn't see the moon and grabbed for the flashlight, which, to her horror, shed a feeble and failing light, the batteries dying even as she watched. Crumpled to the ground, she raised the hood of her sweatshirt against the growing winds and stared as the pinprick of red light vanished. She listened for the creek but could hear nothing over her own breath. She was alone in the woods and lost in the dark.

11
Campfire Companions

Huddled against the nearest tree, Claire reached for the sweatshirt tied about her waist but found the shirt gone. In despair, she moaned with the trees in the wind, their branches cracking, when Moon Doggy rushed to her side. "Moon Doggy!" she shrieked in utter relief, grabbing his neck.

From behind, a sweeping light pierced the darkness ahead, and the beagle slipped from her clutches.

"Where are you, dog?" called a gruff voice from the other side of the tree, and the beagle bounded toward the man.

Instantly Claire recognized the voice. "Jerry, it's me!" she screeched, lunging into the light. For some seconds she stood, hands held before her eyes to shield from its glare, but no one replied. "It's me," she squeaked, suddenly doubtful of who held the light.

"Follow me," the voice commanded.

Claire hesitated until the man shed the light onto his face. "It is you!" she cried in utter relief, scrambling to follow his lead to a campfire outside a sagging, weathered cabin. She thrust her icy hands near the flames while Jerry retrieved a wool blanket, which he draped over her shoulders.

"Now sit on that wood stump and tell me the whole story."

Breathlessly Claire recounted the night's events in the warmth and light of the fire as the old man poured water into a tin pan to heat. Then he settled onto another stump nearby, stroking the beagle's head with one hand and his own gray beard with the other. But when she reached the part of finding Big Red in a cage, his composure dissolved.

"Where?" he cried, pushing the beagle aside to stand. "We've got to save her!"

"I did," Claire said, popping up to face him.

Jerry dropped back down onto the stump, stunned and a bit confused. "You got her out by yourself?" he asked, squinting hard. "She's all right?"

To both questions Claire eagerly nodded, somewhat confused, for how could he think she could do otherwise? "And I know who trapped her, too!" she said, almost boasting.

For a moment or two, he studied her face in the shadow-filled firelight, seeing someone more than a tomboy with white hair and lashes. Here was a stouthearted girl who could wander the woods in moonlight, saving hawks and chasing beagles and owls.

"Okay, then," he said finally, standing again, "tell me who, tell me how, tell me everything!" And he poured the boiling water for tea.

She plunged directly into her encounter with Billy and the horrible discovery of the red-tail, one his father had shot and stuffed. With hand slightly trembling, Jerry extended to Claire a mug of tea. "This hawk," he said, screwing up one eye, "it didn't have a white patch on his forehead, did it?"

Claire closed her eyes to recall the image and opened them again with a start. "Yes, I think it did."

Jerry's head dropped. "I was afraid . . ." his words stalled. For some moments he didn't speak. He sipped from his tea and finally, with an absent gaze, said, "The stuffed hawk—it was Big Red's mate, Mr. Buteo."

Inhaling to calm herself, Claire listened as Jerry explained. For years, Billy's father, Clyde Hollow, had tried but failed to trap Big Red. He was obsessed with killing the hawk, claiming that it stole his aunt's homing pigeons. Claire gasped. Only then did she recall the dead pigeon, still cradled in her sweatshirt pocket.

By the light of a lantern, they buried the pigeon beneath a spruce tree beside the cabin. In a brief tribute over the grave, smelling of fresh earth and tree sap, Jerry said that her name was Powder, the fastest-flying and favorite pigeon of his late friend Mike.

Neither again mentioned Clyde that night, his name too despicable to utter in the wake of a sacred ceremony. Claire slept by the fire in a sleeping bag and awoke three hours later to Moon Doggy draped over her legs and a bowl of oatmeal thrust into her face.

"Get up," Jerry said. On his shoulder perched Becky, preening her red feathers.

"Becky! Where was she last night?" Claire asked, yawning.

"Settled for the night inside the cabin. Now hurry, else your mother will wake before we get you back."

Claire ate while Jerry put out the fire. Then, with beagle and chicken, they set out in the predawn twilight.

A gray sky grazed the treetops as they walked through veils of ghostly mist, sweetly scented. Above the creek, she prepared to go on alone.

"I'll take Moon Doggy back," he said, grabbing the beagle's collar. "And I'll get Mr. Buteo a proper burial."

"But he's in that shed—"

"I'll get 'im," Jerry said decisively, suddenly preoccupied with her eyes, which she quickly averted. "Hey, don't look away," he said, grabbing her chin. "I couldn't tell last night 'cause of the firelight." And after a brief examination he

❧ An Odd Bird ❦

summarily said, "So you're different. Thank God and stop being silly."

Claire said not another word but plunged down the ridge toward the creek. She trod alongside the rolling waters, thinking only of what Jerry had said: "thank God and stop being silly." How could he think her silly for being embarrassed? She was, after all, a kind of freak.

At first she didn't notice the drifting lacey snowflakes until a few flakes collected on her eyebrows. Looking out into the gently falling snow, she spotted something in the distance, cradled in the forking trunk of a white pine.

"Could it be?" she whispered, quietly approached the sleeping owl. Claire noted the circular rings framing a heart-shaped face and vertical bars striping a creamy chest and knew this was the stocky, round-headed barred owl.

Only feet away, she stopped to rudely gawk. Just then, the owl opened his heavy-lashed eyelids, revealing dark brown eyes. He looked down into Claire's golden eyes, locking stares with the girl for some seconds. Then, as a semitransparent membrane slid diagonally across his eyes, he turned his head away. Claire took the cue that the visit was over. But as she moved away, the owl again opened his dark eyes, following her with his head.

"It was nice to finally meet you," she called back to him, walking through the falling snow of a perfect world where a girl could meet an owl at dawn.

On the bus to school that morning, Victor was not happy to hear Claire announce that she had walked Moon Doggy at midnight. "Why didn't you tell me!" he scolded, his warm brown eyes suddenly cold. "I'm the one who wanted to go on a midnight walk with the dog!"

"But you're grounded," she protested.

"Not at midnight!" cried Victor. "My mother would be asleep; she'd never know!" Too angry to talk, he stared into the aisle as Claire fought to keep from crying. Her only friend was turning against her, a little each day.

"We'll go together next month, I promise," she said.

"I'll go on my own," he answered, standing, "and when I want to. He stomped up the aisle, dropping heavily into another seat.

Now Claire, too, was angry. Victor hadn't given her a chance to tell about Big Red—how she had saved her from the trap. She would never tell him; he didn't deserve to know. He had already taken sides against her with Billy, who awaited Victor at the curb to claim him. Staring through the bus window, Claire sought Billy's exposed eye, always roving because it carried the work of two. How she wished that his stupid hair, worn like a patch over his right eye, would blow from his forehead to expose it.

12
Earth Magic

That night, Sammy slumped to the bedside rug with a grunt of protest. Claire was in bed at eight o'clock, exhausted from her escapades of the prior night. From wakefulness she slipped into slumber where once again she stood before the barred owl.

"Is it okay if I tell him?"

Tell WHO what?

"Tell Victor about you and me."

What about you and me?

"That we're special friends."

We only just met.

"I mean about our secret."

The owl's inner lids slid sideways over his eyes, a message that the exchange was over.

Of her many dreams that long night, Claire remembered only that the barred owl would not answer her question. She bit into the pillow cradling her chin. Would Victor speak to her today? Or would he again ignore her? She didn't know but suspected Billy as the source of his contrary moods.

In the front yard, she waited for the school bus. Flaming leaves swirled about her on crisp air currents while hotter emotions swirled within. On this day, she wore no bird image, an ongoing experiment to see if she could attract birds with only her will. But she had forgotten to pick a bird, at random, from a deck of birding flash cards. No matter, she thought, biting her lower lip. I'll just pick one from my head.

The colorful fall morning blared adventure in every flying bird and fluttering leaf. The chill air excited her senses. Looking up the road for the bus, she felt an urge to flee. Inside the house, Sammy stood upright behind the bay window, wooly head tilted quizzically, paws propped on its sill, tail wagging. He seemed to read her mind. *Yes, let's go!* he said, pushing off from the sill to lunge for the front door, which she threw open. "Come on, Sammy!" she cried, urgent to escape. They must make it to the woods before the bus took the hairpin curve above the hollow. They bolted over the road and through the downward-sloping pasture toward the woodland and creek.

Freedom!

Sammy set the mood, frantic for exploration and fun. While he plunged into the water hole, she dumped the heavy contents of her book bag creekside but for the packed lunch and beverage. Without books on her back, she almost floated over the stepping-stones. Sammy surged from the water and charged past her on the deer path cut diagonally across the elevation. At the top, she looked down upon the woodland creek bordering their property. Beyond it lay adventure—and trespass—as the common raven, a large ebony bird, reminded her:

Krunnnkkk! Krunnnkkk! This territory is taken! Get along! Get along!

"Oh!" Claire caught but a glimpse of the hawk-like bird sailing over hemlocks swaying in the wind. He reminded her of something else: "I forgot to pick a bird!" But should she pick one after twice forgetting? That hardly seemed scientific, and this was an experiment. Far ahead, along a corridor of red and yellow falling leaves, Sammy stopped to shake water from his soggy coat. "Wait for me!" she cried, an image filling her mind. "We're looking for a ring-necked pheasant!"

Autumn was the season of falling leaves and departures. Birds of all species who did not live in Pennsylvania year-round were migrating to wintering grounds. Soon, mostly year-round resident birds would remain, and among them was the ring-necked pheasant.

Ahead, Sammy set a course toward the widow's property. Fifty feet behind, Claire ambled after, spinning slowly with the wind, arms aloft like wings, face tilted to the canopy overhead. She and Sammy knew this woodland path, high above the creek, because they traveled it daily, a highway into a magical world. As with the twist of a kaleidoscope, the green woodland had erupted with color. Once-green ferns now swept the forest with bronzy shades. Grass stalks in open areas glowed creamy gold and stands of sumac burned bright red with berries. Within a grove of mature hemlock Sammy stopped to wait for her until his nose caught a strong scent. Then he was off, bounding into a wild and open tangle of vegetation. Old tree snags plastered with dried grasses or choked with vines littered the woodland opening. Prickly shrubs and hidden ground holes checked any impulse she might have to follow. She continued along the cultivated deer path.

At the hemlock grove Claire drifted into a strong odor of buck urine, the current of scent that had carried off Sammy. It was an interesting smell, pungent and musky, yet she liked it, even took a big draft into her lungs. Then she headed toward the old logging road winding downward to the hollow and creek. The route they had begun was a circuit, one that would lead them home again or to Helen's property, but she had other ideas. All along the creekside grew the tall and gangly tree-shrub rhododendron. Crawling among a jumble of its contorted branches, she sat on the creekbank to wait for Sammy. Watching the cold flowing water, untouched by the rising sun, she let her mind wander.

Two nights before, she had chased Moon Doggy down from Helen's property to the opposite bank of this creek. Fading scratches still traced her palms. How incredible that she had followed the beagle into the night. Even more incredible that, when lost and desperate, she should find the Chicken Man: Jerry. He was not a raving lunatic after all; even so, he was odd, really odd. Up the hillside behind her, she had first discovered the scruffy old man under a hemlock with his chicken. A sudden thought made her shudder: had he been waiting for her under that hemlock? She came this way every day; maybe he had been watching her every day. With a quickening pulse, she reviewed their subsequent meeting. She and Victor had chased after him . . . or had he led them to the outcrop? Three seemingly coincidental incidents. But now they seemed as coincidental as the birds who daily found her.

The ring-necked pheasant! Yet again, she had forgotten. She climbed to her feet with a plan for her stolen day: find both the Chicken Man and the pheasant. She squeezed through the twisting thickets of rhododendron, whose limbs held her as within a cage. Free, finally, she called for Sammy: Hoo hoo ho-ho, hoo hoo ho-hoooooaw! Hoo hoo ho-ho, hoo hoo ho-hoooooaw! From the hillside, he came bounding into view down the logging road. The sight of him always filled her with joy—a big-headed, black-nosed bulk of wooly fur charging toward her with wild enthusiasm. He whipped past, splashing into the creek where its banks were lowest, nearly level with the ground. On the opposite side, he twisted back, large tongue lolling from his panting mouth. She was hopping across a bridge of small boulders. "Come on, boy! We're heading someplace new."

Though Claire directed the route change, Sammy led the way, trotting downstream, nose scouring the ground. He had picked up the scent of the beagle. How lucky! Now they'd have no trouble finding the camp of the Chicken Man.

13
Becky and Her Boyfriend

Claire followed Sammy along the creek, whose banks rose higher and higher, its waters choked with large boulders. This was no tame creek to cross on stepping-stones. She kept distant from its ledge, marveling at the doom that might have befallen her when chasing through the dark after Moon Doggy. Her body retained some memory of moving over this landscape—the level stretches, basins, and inclines. She felt familiarity with it through her limbs if not eyes.

When scaling a low ridge, Claire suspected the camp site would be near. Any doubt disappeared when she saw Sammy, upright on hind legs, straining against a tree trunk for sight or scent of some animal. "The porcupine tree!" She bolted forward to pace beneath the black oak. A fragrance of wood-burning smoke led her onward to where, in the distance, stood the squat, weathered cabin. She had intended to approach stealthily, but Sammy rushed ahead, barking excitedly.

Jerry sat on a tree stump, prodding the logs of a dying fire with a short metal pole. On either shoulder perched a nervous pigeon, preparing to fly from the dog. Uttering calming words to his birds, Jerry stood to intercept the rollicking canine. "Down," he commanded of the sheepdog bouncing up on hind legs. Sammy dropped to all fours. "Sit." Sammy sat, tail wagging.

"How did you do that?" Claire hurried forward to join them. Three sets of eyes turned to greet her. "I can never get him to listen," she said to the middle set, glancing between his head-side companions.

"It's in the tone of voice," Jerry said in the same low octave, but with smiling eyes for Claire. "Now sit on that stump." He pointed to one across the fire ring. "Take your dog," he added as she twisted away. "I'll get you a cup of coffee."

Like an obedient dog, Sammy followed Claire and sat beside her, though sniffing for the pigeons. Claire, too, felt obedient, though she had come to discover some secret agenda of the man she alternately thought of as Jerry or the Chicken Man. For now, he was Jerry.

"These are your pigeons?" she said, accepting a tin cup with black coffee, something she never drank at home, but here appropriate, even good, especially with double sugar.

"Yes, this is Patty." He nodded to the stout-bodied pigeon on his right, a black-and-white or "pied" bird. "And this is Peggy." He nodded to the pigeon on his left, a gray-and-black bird with an iridescent green head. She bobbed it as in greeting. "They live with Mike's pigeons, but I fetch them out every other day or so for a good airing."

"Does Helen know?"

"Of course not." He chuckled. "When will you get it through your head? She don't like me."

"It just seems odd how you can come and go on her property without getting caught." She patted Sammy's head while sipping the coffee. "That loft is in sight of the kitchen window. And don't they miss the birds when you take them?"

Sitting back down onto his stump, Jerry assured her that Helen or Clyde had little occasion to miss the birds. And that he, not Clyde, regularly cleaned the loft. Yet another astonishing revelation for Claire. To her, he must be a magician of sorts to so frequently avoid discovery. His secretive existence added to her growing suspicions that she, too, was ignorant of his designs. She needed to know more about him.

❧ Becky and Her Boyfriend ❦

"Helen says that you baked pies for old man Kelly."

"Did she?" He wagged a finger alongside his shaggy, whiskered face, and both pigeons at once flew from his shoulder and into the air. Sammy jumped to attention, watching them. "That was in an old life." He stared into his coffee. All remained quiet but the cooing birds now atop the cabin roof.

"My mother and I live in Kelly's old house." '

His head snapped upright. "Is that so?"

"Yes. And we're opening a small grocery, just like Kelly."

Jerry stared at her but did not see her, hazel eyes cast upon some internal image or calculation. She waited for his attention, abruptly delivered and altogether off topic. "Why aren't you in school today?"

She ignored his question. "Where's Becky?"

As if summoned, the rusty-red chicken scampered on bright yellow legs into sight from somewhere behind her. Claire grabbed Sammy's collar while Becky bounced with flapping wings to the perch of Jerry's shoulder, tail end rocking back and forth for balance. Then she traced behind his neck, popping alongside his ear to stare out with dazzling flame-orange eyes. Becky's spectacular entrance distracted all attention from the unlikely companion trailing behind: a ring-necked pheasant! This long-tailed escort strutted directly past Sammy, still straining to smell Becky. Not until he stood squarely among the onlookers did anyone notice him, a regal bird with a flashy green head; red face; and luxurious, thick white collar.

"Henry!" cried Jerry, hoisting urgently upward to snatch the bird before Sammy did. In the cradle of Jerry's arm, the coppery-colored pheasant appeared completely at ease despite the bustle. Looking upward to Jerry, the pheasant then cast his yellow-brown eyes to the astounded onlookers.

"Meet Henry," Jerry said. "He's a friend of Becky's."

Claire stared at Jerry who held a pheasant while a chicken perched upon his shoulder. Overhead two pigeons peered down upon him from the roof gable. Clearly, he was more than a "Chicken Man."

"I didn't know you had a pet pheasant," she said, wondering if Henry could count as a "sighting" in her experiment.

"Henry's no pet," said Jerry, insulted for the pheasant. "He's wild." His mood abruptly changed. "Get going with that dog now," he ordered. "I need to let these two down."

Claire did not take too much offense, given her experience with his changing nature. Getting a good grip on Sammy's leash, she stood up to leave. "I almost forgot to tell you! I saw Big Red the other day, when I was riding my bicycle on Kelly Store Road." This bit of news yet again changed his disposition from surly to happily surprised.

"Did you? So . . . details."

Claire explained how the hawk descended from the sky to fly directly overhead while she "flew" below on her bicycle with outstretched arms.

"Imagine that," he said as much to himself as to her. "Did she say anything?" For an instant he held an expectant expression until realizing his error. "I mean did you say anything—to others—about her."

"Yes, I told Victor, but he didn't seem to care. In that instant, Claire decided to tell Jerry of her odd visual experiences, first with Big Red and then with the red-bellied woodpecker. If anyone would understand becoming invisible, he would, but Sammy began straining at the leash and Becky squawking in defense. So, hesitantly, she turned to head home. On route she devised a story for her mother about missing the bus to chase Sammy who had bolted from the door and into the woods.

On the following day, Claire returned from school to find her mother unpacking groceries in the kitchen. Swinging shut the refrigerator door, she eagerly told of a strange man walking down Kelly Store Road with a chicken on his shoulder. Alarm flashed over Claire's face, but her mother saw only surprise and continued unpacking the groceries.

"Not only that," she said, "the old man winked and waved at me!" She chuckled with the novelty. "Well, because it was raining, and he looked so harmless, I offered him a ride, never thinking that the chicken would roost on my seat back!"

Her mother further reported that the old man used to bake pies for Kelly. Claire almost spurted out "I know!" but caught herself as her mother paused to pose a question. "How antiseptic could his kitchen be with a chicken running loose?" Taking a much-needed breath, she looked, smiling, to her daughter.

Claire could think to say only one thing: "Do you think his pies are any good?"

That question was unexpectedly answered when the baker himself arrived at their door on Saturday morning, one week before the store's grand opening. Claire gawked to see the Chicken Man, Jerry, standing before her, apple pie in hand. His wooly hair had been cut short, though still kinky, his scruffy beard trimmed to a close turf of whiskers, his dirty overalls exchanged for khaki pants and a button-up shirt. He looked (and smelled) entirely presentable.

"Jerry!" she said much too loudly.

He tapped a finger to his lips. "Let's keep our acquaintance secret for now."

"Mom!" she hollered into the house. "A man with a pie is at the door!"

14
Defending Her Own

The morning of the grand store opening was cold and gray, with clouds flowing overhead like a wide, rushing river. All week long the new and improved Jerry had visited each day with another pie to demonstrate his talents and to earn a customer. He and pies were delivered to their door by old man Tucker, a tall, lanky, scant-haired man who ran an unofficial taxi service from his 1985 Chevy Impala. This morning Jerry arrived early with six pies. Now he and Louise were busy in the store preparing a bake sale display on a central table. Meanwhile, Claire sat outside, across the road under the large oak, brooding and watching her hot breath rise as clouds in the air.

"It's not fair," she said, pouting, as Sammy patrolled a neighboring oak, up which he had just chased a squirrel. "Jerry was my friend first." She had good reason to mope. Not only had Jerry seemingly forgotten her but so had Victor, who sat with her only sometimes on the bus. And when he did, they never—ever—spoke of Billy. But for Sammy and the birds, she felt forsaken.

Kree-eeer-ar . . . kree-eeer-ar . . . kree-eeer-ar . . .

Soaring high above the tree line was Big Red! From the ground she jumped and hurried into the open pasture, binoculars ready. The blurred image of Big Red sharpened and grew with a twist of the focus knob. Claire could see her searching brown eyes. Did those eyes yet seek her missing mate, not knowing his horrible end? With rhythmic strokes, the raptor called again and again, etching a wide circle above her in the sky. Claire felt these calls were meant for her. Then, leaving the loop, Big Red flew along the woodland edge toward the widow Whiner's, and Claire ran below to follow.

Angry dark clouds seemed to skim the treetops. Heading against the motion of their current felt like walking upstream, though no winds scoured the ground. Time and again she stopped to wait for Sammy, but hearing nothing, hurried on without him. She approached the widow's property from behind, through the woods. In the distance, a man yelled, and Claire ducked. She could see the back of the widow's house. Between it and the pigeon loft stood a man wearing work overalls, yelling toward the house.

"Who's been in my work shed?!" he demanded.

Claire slipped closer to the scene, dodging among young, bushy hemlocks. On to the side porch, the widow suddenly appeared.

"Shut your trap, Clyde!" she barked. "What do I want with that stupid shed?" and marched backed into the kitchen with the screen door snapping behind. Claire immediately understood. Billy's father had just discovered his missing trophy: Mr. Buteo, the stuffed and mounted red-tail that Jerry had taken to bury. Clyde threw his work cap to the ground and stormed toward the shed, his furious mood mirrored by an ever-lowering sky.

The soft cooing of pigeons drew her eyes to the loft roof, where two strutted nervously; two more perched on the branch of a young oak. If the pigeons were out, then Billy's father was cleaning the loft. As a wind began to blow, the pair in the oak flew directly over Claire, lighting in a locust tree where the woodland met the pasture. Through binoculars she watched the pretty pair preen and stretch their wings. But the field of view held something else, a speck far off in the heavy dark sky: a hawk.

Hearing the utility shed door slam, Claire ducked behind the tree's wind-whipped branches. Clyde retrieved his discarded cap from the ground, stood, and threw back his head to vent fury into the sky: "Who the hell was in my shed?"

Swaying like one of the windswept trees, he stood rooted to the spot, while Claire gawked, astonished by his anguish.

"He must be drunk," she whispered to herself.

Finally, he lurched toward the side of the house and his truck. Claire sighed with relief; he was leaving. But each turn of the ignition key produced a hollow whir. Clyde spilled from the truck door, cursing. And Claire turned to run back toward the creek until she heard the territorial cry of a red-tail.

Soaring in smaller and smaller circles, the hawk was slowly migrating toward the woodland's edge, where the two pigeons flew from the locust tree to the top of the barn, as if preparing a flight plan of their own. Big Red was a fierce predator, not content simply with snakes and small rodents. She had a taste for chicken or pigeon and would steal these from humans. Though free to soar, she was a fugitive from those who would shoot her from the sky for such offenses. And there were those whose envy of her power and beauty drove them to hunt her for a trophy, as did Billy's father. Now predator and hunter drew nearer, unaware of the other.

While Billy's father opened the creaking hood of the truck, Big Red soared closer to the woodland's edge, and the worried pigeons waddled nervously over the tin barn roof. With binoculars, Claire watched the raptor, buffeted by the winds, descend until a few hundred feet above ground, where she leveled, heading straight toward the barn. Transfixed, Claire held the hawk's head directly within her field of view. It was as if she herself were the hawk and felt within her own breast the primal cry,

Kree-eeer-ar . . . kree-eeer-ar . . . kree-eeer-ar . . .

The sound of a slamming truck door sounded distant and hollow; only the raptor filled Claire's senses as it eventually dove toward the barn roof where startled pigeons flew into the air.

"Merry Christmas to me!"

Claire heard these words as if through a megaphone, followed by a horrible blast—a shotgun blast. Hawk and pigeons froze in midair; then one pigeon fell, dropping onto the barn roof with a thud, as the raptor swept upward. Claire was on her feet, a rock in her hand, flung at the man who took second aim. Her missile struck his head, his shotgun jumping into the air as it discharged—CRACK-K-K-K!

The stunned man stumbled backward as Big Red disappeared over the treetops. "What?" he muttered, seeing the strange pale figure standing defiantly before him, only half a dozen yards away, the shotgun slipping from his grasp and falling onto the ground.

"I'm going to report you!" Claire shouted, charging him. "You can't shoot red-tails!"

"Did you hit me with that rock?" he said, befuddled, rubbing his temple.

Claire stared into his face, which looked nothing like she expected. His features were delicate, not brutish; his complexion fair, not dark. But his eyes were bloodshot and face unshaven for many days.

"And I know about Mr. Buteo, too," she said, ignoring his question.

Clyde shook his head, confused but becoming annoyed. "Did you throw that rock at me?"

"You killed and stuffed Big Red's mate!" Claire felt like pounding his chest with her fists.

Instantly Clyde understood, his eyes shifting in thought.

"And you tried to shoot Big Red," she said, "so I'm telling the police!"

"Hold on there, missy," he grabbed her arm as she passed. "Not so fast."

Claire violently ripped her arm free.

"I need your name," he said, sneering, and she could see a huge gap between his front teeth. "The police will want to know who assaulted me." He squatted to retrieve the rock she had thrown. Wrapping it in a greasy handkerchief, he said, "Evidence."

Claire wanted to shove him hard—knock him over and grab the "evidence"—and maybe would have if not for Helen, whose sudden presence behind them destroyed all opportunity.

"What the devil are you two doing?!" she yelled.

"I was scaring off a hawk from the pigeons is all, so git back to the house."

"But Claire," the widow pleaded, hugging herself against the cold, "what are you doing here with Clyde?"

Claire glanced at the rock held inconspicuously by Billy's father and then at his forehead, where a visible lump was forming. Seeing her dismay, he pulled his cap down farther to conceal the swelling, wincing with the discomfort. Claire listened to herself lie to the widow.

"Sammy took off again, Mrs. Whiner, and I was looking for him here."

"Well, where is he, then?"

"I haven't found him yet," Claire said, flushing with shame, because in that instant, she and Billy's father had

An Odd Bird

become conspirators, together withholding the truth from Helen. And as she walked back to the house with the widow, she and Clyde knew that neither would act on their own threats because both had something to hide.

15
The Missed Call

Hurrying down the widow's winding drive, Claire headed toward the road, the quickest way home. The morning's dark clouds had lifted, revealing a white-gray atmosphere, where sky and air seemed one. She jogged along the road bordering their pasture, looking down toward her own home, only a short distance away.

She bounded up the store's porch just as a small red sedan pulled into the graveled lot, big enough for only four cars. She burst through the door expecting everyone's full attention but could see that both her mother and Jerry were looking beyond her to the coming customer. "Not right now, Claire," Louise said, even before Claire had uttered a word. And a beseeching look to Jerry went unnoticed as he walked past to greet the stranger behind. She wanted to yell out for everyone to hear: Clyde Hallow killed a pigeon! He tried to kill Big Red, but I hit him with a rock! Yet she couldn't ruin her mother's big opening. And she couldn't confess to physical violence. Instead she skulked away, pushing through the swinging door into their living room.

Only Sammy could make her feel better, so she rushed through the downstairs and then hurried up the stairwell to see if he had come home. He hadn't—unless he lay somewhere in the yard. Back down the stairwell and through the summer kitchen, she spilled outside, where a light snow was falling.

"Sammy!" she called, taking a lap around the house. Turning its corner, she nearly collided with a battered green pickup pulling into the lot. On her toes she teetered an instant as the truck brushed by and pulled to a stop, belching black exhaust in her face. "Oh, no!" thought Claire. "It can't be like this—it can't!" The idea of strange people coming and going into her house all day was intolerable. She sought the sanctuary of her own bedroom, plunging her head under a pillow. She quickly slipped into sleep and lazily awoke two hours later with a smile on her face, reaching bedside to stroke Sammy, but he wasn't there. Straightaway she jumped up and hurried downstairs into the storeroom. There she found her mother and Jerry sipping hot tea at a small table by the window. Relieved to find no rude strangers in their house, Claire asked urgently, "Where's Sammy?"

"Were you sleeping?" Louise said.

"Mom, is Sammy here or not?"

"Helen Whiner called just a bit ago to say she's got him again."

"Why didn't you get me?" Claire snapped. "How long ago did she call?"

"Don't get snippy," her mother said sternly, yet couldn't help but smile, so gratified was she with the day's success. "And you'll never believe who came into the store—Victor's father, George Arquetana."

At any other time, this news would have enticed Claire, but not now. "That's great, but how long ago did she call?"

"Listen for a minute, will you?" Louise glanced at Jerry long enough to roll her eyes. "I recognized Mr. Arquetana—he was the man who found you as a lost little girl under that tree!"

"Victor's father? He found me?"

"Yes!" Louise clasped her hands. "Isn't that something?"

But Claire didn't know what to say, afraid to let slip one of the many secrets kept from her mother. Throughout her childhood, her mother had told Claire the bedtime story of a little girl lost in the woods but found by a beautiful hawk and a kind man. It was their very own fairy tale. Now the characters were back in their lives, which must mean that they were living the tale, not just remembering it.

"You have to tell me everything—every word!" Claire said, "but wait till I get back with Sammy."

Three inches of dry snow had fallen during Claire's nap, so she bundled up with hat, coat, gloves, and boots. The snow would not clump but slid through her gloved fist like silky sand. She skidded across the road toward the oak above the creek, thinking of the many recent changes in her life. From the large oak, she skidded and slid down to the creek, whose icy water rolled between snow-covered banks. Climbing the steep ridge beyond the creek proved difficult in the slippery snow. Only by anchoring her feet against rocks, roots, or the woody stems of rhododendron could she hoist herself up the incline.

At the ridgetop, just as she stood from her climb, Claire saw a large black-and-white bird with a two-foot wingspan and fire engine red crest—a pileated woodpecker. With slow, rowing wings he flew just fifty feet away, along a wide, treeless corridor.

Kuk kuk keekeekeekeekeekeekuk kuk! He shrieked a territorial call of sharp, accelerating notes and was gone. Like the barred owl, this huge woodpecker was no stranger to Claire, who heard his drumming on occasion but seldom caught sight of him, which is why beneath her wool coat she wore a white sweater recently embossed with the pileated's image. However, Claire neither scouted nor listened for birds but hurried toward the widow's. An anxious Mrs. Whiner met her on the side porch, looking somewhat deranged. The bobby pins, typically plastered against her head, floated above it on loosened coils of wispy hair. With boney fingers, the widow plowed her scalp like furrows in a field.

"Billy's taken Sammy!" she cried. "Where have you been?"

"What?" Claire ran to the opposite side of the house, where the widow had once tied Sammy, but he wasn't there. Then she ran back, grabbing onto the step railing to keep from flying past.

"Where?" she panted. "Where did he take him?"

The widow shook her head, looking in the direction of the barn. Some of the bobby pins now drooped over her forehead. "He said he recognized the sheepdog, knew who it belonged to, and was taking him back."

"He belongs to me!" Claire screamed, tears filling her eyes.

"I know, child; I know." The widow extended a hand to Claire, but she backed away.

"When?" Claire sobbed.

"I kept calling but the phone was busy and busy and busy."

"When? When did he take him?"

"Must be an hour now," Helen muttered. "Girl, I would've walked down to the house but for the snow."

"Snow!" Claire cried, looking at her own fresh tracks. "Did they walk?"

The widow pointed toward the barn and Claire dashed away, heedless of all else but her dog.

16
Lost in the Snow

The snow fell more heavily now, insulating the world in white tranquility—but to Claire it was a gift and a curse, providing tracks for her to follow but also obliterating those same tracks. At the doghouse, imprinted in the snow, was a shuffle of feet and paws, already softened into gentle waves. Claire followed the stream of rippling snow out into the pasture that fronted the barn.

Dismayed at how quickly the snow was erasing their trail, Claire pushed faster, plowing fresh snow to use as her and Sammy's trail back. At about thirty acres, the pasture was a long rectangle, enclosed on three sides by woods. Through the blinding white storm, she could not see ahead to determine which direction the trail led, whether straight across the vast snow-covered field or off into the woodland bordering either side. Like a dog following a scent, she kept her head locked to the ground ahead. These tracks were already an hour old, but fresher ones would lie ahead, if only she could breach the distance between them in less time than it took Billy. Time was Claire's enemy; to battle it she must run. Pumping her legs harder, she moved from a jogging pace to a full stride. The snow was much wetter now, tugging at each footfall, and her legs soon felt the strain.

Through the white haze she saw a gray backdrop, the woodland's edge. The trail was veering toward the woods, and once inside the tree line, the world again came into focus. Emerald hemlock, rugged oak, graceful birch, these and other trees greeted her as she wound through them following the trail. In places sheltered by hemlock, the snow was less deep and Billy's trail more defined.

Tiring now, Claire stumbled over a knotty tree root or fallen branch and spilled into the wet snow, sitting for a few seconds to rest before rising to go on. Her thighs were wet and cold from snow and her feet burned, but otherwise she felt overly hot and would throw off her hat, only to pull it on moments later.

As her progress slowed, Claire thought more about what she might encounter at the trail's end, especially as she passed the shells of rusting cars, lying among the trees like skeletons. And then to her horror, just ahead, sat an orange school bus, without wheels but yet not abandoned. Sagging curtains hung from a string across some of the windows, and white plastic bags full of garbage lay propped near the bus doors. Claire grabbed her breath and stopped in midstride. Was someone in that bus this moment, watching her approach?

Though the trail led directly past the bus windows, Claire stepped backward, turning to retrace her own path until finding the cover of a young, wide hemlock. For a few moments she watched the bus, awaiting someone to descend its steps to chase after her. But no one did. With pounding heart, she headed away and around the bus, looking to intersect Billy and Sammy's trail somewhere ahead.

With the bus well behind her now, she scoured a wide area, looking for the trail that was not to be found. Seized with dread, Claire pushed back toward the bus and then noticed it. Swinging down from a pole behind the rusting orange hulk was an electric line. She followed it with cold, aching feet, knowing that the line would connect with another pole or maybe—hopefully—a building.

🙞 Lost in the Snow 🙜

She stumbled repeatedly toward a second pole that led her to a small clearing within which stood a two-story concrete block building. Was this someone's house? All manner of junk littered the backyard, though the deepening mantle of snow obscured most but for a stove, its oven door flung open, and a bench seat of a car. Smoke rose from the building's chimney and yellow light shone from a few of the downstairs windows. And at once her predicament became apparent: not only had she lost Sammy's trail, but also she herself was lost. Her toes burned, the pant legs of frozen jeans scraped against her numb thighs, and she shivered with cold. She had to ask for help.

Trudging toward the side of the house, she glanced at the woodland facing it and stopped. Tucked between the front row of trees were half a dozen doghouses. Claire scanned these, each with an occupant hidden within, away from cold and wet, but for the last. Outside the last house sat a large dog, completely covered by snow, at the end of his short chain. He stared intently at the windows of the lit house, unaware of her.

In one glance she knew. "Sammy!"

Her voice broke the spell. Perking up his ears, he jerked his head in her direction as she dashed toward him.

"Sammy!" she cried. "Sammy!"

Like a patient child he sat, tail wagging wildly, scraping a trough in the snow.

"Don't bark; please don't bark!" she urged, rushing toward him, but her advice was lost on Sammy's neighbors, who, spilling from their houses, began a chorus of well-rehearsed barking.

Tearing her gloves off with her teeth, Claire switched her plans from a plea for help to a rescue and escape. She had to get Sammy free and away from the building before anyone tried to stop her. Thankfully the connecting latch was easy to unhinge, and in an instant the two were bounding past the other dogs, straining madly against their own lines, barking fiercely against the unfairness of being left behind.

Claire headed directly toward the truck parked beside the house; they would follow the driveway to whatever lane or road it attached. But, of course, there was no visible road to follow. All was covered in five inches of undisturbed snow. Sammy needed no urging to keep by Claire's side. When she stopped, he stopped.

"Shut up, you stinking dogs!" bellowed a man from the door. Claire and Sammy jolted into motion as one, following a wide treeless corridor running in front of the house. Whatever her discomforts moments earlier, Claire felt nothing but hot blood propelling her through drifting snow, creating a furrow within which Sammy now followed. A couple hundred feet away was a bend in the lane, where they would rest when out of sight of the concrete house.

Once there, Claire crumpled to the ground, grabbing Sammy to squeeze him hard, as hard as the pain of losing him. The chained dogs had quieted under threat of abuse, and the moment was still. Hot tears flowed over Claire's frozen cheeks as she pulled back to survey her beloved Sammy. More than snow covered him; balls of ice, some the size of golf balls, hung from his fur. Tugging on these to pull them free, she dodged Sammy's warm tongue seeking her salty tears.

"Look at you!" she said over and over again. "Just look at you." And when her hands were too cold to continue, she forced them into her wet gloves to start again. But rising to leave, Claire discovered that the ice balls hanging from Sammy's fur were of small consequence—that is, compared to those crippling him. As she started their trudging trek, Sammy

Lost in the Snow

could only hobble behind, so she stopped to check his paws and found dozens of hard ice pellets crowding his footpads.

Slumping again into the snow, she set to work dislodging these with her bare fingers and finally resorted to crushing them with her teeth. Thereafter the task went much more quickly. Soon they were up again and moving down the lane, which branched onto a plowed road just ahead.

Now in the dim twilight before dark, the two stood roadside, deciding which way to head. In the distance, they saw the headlights of a car. Stepping farther into the road, she saw that it was their own green coup wagon! It pulled slowly alongside and stopped, and Louise spilled out onto the ground in her haste.

"Claire!" she cried, struggling to stand, while Jerry rushed across the headlights to aid her.

"We're okay, Mom!" Claire said, crying as she helped her mother stand.

Louise hugged her hard, while Jerry opened the backseat for Sammy to jump in, saying, "Okay, let's get this family home."

17
One Survives

Claire sank her red, chafed skin into the soothing warm bathwater as her mother went downstairs to make supper. Meanwhile, in the summer kitchen, Jerry attended to Sammy with a towel, having first to dunk each paw in a bucket of warm water to melt the ice pellets embedded in his footpads. Later, as Louise stirred a marinara sauce on the stove, Claire sipped tea quietly until Jerry and Sammy blundered in from the summer kitchen. Sammy nearly knocked the cup from her hands with his big, freshly toweled head.

"You had quite an adventure today, little lady," Jerry said, winking, as he pulled out a chair to sit. He seemed so comfortable and happy, as though he had always sat at their table. And because of the heavy snow and late hour, her mother had invited him to spend the night in their guest room. Louise made Claire tell the story in painstaking detail, interrupting all the while with questions. But when Claire described how Billy's father had shot the pigeon and she had thrown the rock, Louise dropped her stirring spoon, splattering marinara sauce all over the floor.

"Did he hurt you?" she cried, pulling Claire's chair out from the table to face her.

Claire assured her he had not as Jerry wiped the sauce from the floor, with help from Sammy and his discriminating tongue.

Then Louise fretted over possible legal action against Claire, asking Jerry a host of questions until finally he said,

✥ One Survives ✥

"Listen. Clyde Hollow ain't going to report that some little girl hit him with a rock."

"But shouldn't we report him?" piped Claire.

"No," he said firmly, grabbing a piece of bread to butter. Claire waited for an explanation as his face sagged. "Me and my friend Mike—the widow's husband—were like a couple of kids, sending messages to each other by pigeon." He had become suddenly nostalgic. "I would keep a few of Mike's pigeons at my loft and he would keep mine at his, and whenever we wanted to send word to the other, we'd band a note to the pigeon's leg and set him free to fly home. Pigeons are trained to fly home."

"Oh," said Claire. "Then the widow's pigeons won't fly off when out of the loft because they're already home."

"That's right, but my pigeons"—his fork sagged over the plate—"I mean my pigeon—those two you spoke of on the barn roof were likely mine—will fly home to my loft."

"You mean," Claire said, stopping to look for guidance from her mother, who bowed her head sympathetically. "You mean," Claire softly said, looking again to him, "the pigeon he shot was yours?"

He nodded. No one spoke for some seconds as Claire frantically searched for a less mournful topic but could think of nothing but pigeons. "I didn't know you had a loft at the cabin."

A bit embarrassed, he stood, picking up his empty plate. "I fixed up one inside the cabin." He deposited it in the sink and glanced over his shoulder. "In a separate area, of course." He chuckled nervously. "They can't perch on my kitchen table or anything."

The next day, Claire woke to a sunny morning, the snow outside shining with blue-white brilliance. Over breakfast, they discussed plans for snow removal, after which each would be free to pursue his or her Sunday. When Jerry announced his intention to hike to his cabin to retrieve Becky and the surviving pigeon, Claire pleaded to go along, but her mother suggested a different plan. She would drive them as close as possible and wait while they hiked in for the birds. Then she would drive Jerry to his home in town. Louise lent Jerry her snow boots, though they were a bit big for him, for the trek back to his cabin. An access lane used by another family had been plowed, but the rutted track to Jerry's cabin was a glistening white ribbon of undisturbed snow. Yet Jerry and Claire trudged through it with single-minded purpose: to retrieve Becky and the surviving pigeon.

"Do you think your pigeons—I mean, pigeon—got to the cabin okay?" she asked.

"Yep. I bet she's perched cozy right alongside Becky."

"Do you think she knows? I mean that the other pigeon got killed?"

"I can't say, Claire, but at least Becky's with her."

The two moved more quickly and soon the cabin, huddled under six inches of snow, came into view.

"Mind that fire ring," Jerry said as Claire strode eagerly toward the door. "You'll trip over the rocks."

Noting the gentle bulging outline of its circle, she hopped around and opened the cabin door. As daylight flooded in, the smell of wet feathers rolled out. And there, poised expectantly on the kitchen table (despite Jerry's claims to the contrary), stood Becky and the pigeon.

From behind her, Jerry cried "Patty!" his voice filled with relief and regret. "Patty, my girl," he said, extending his arm for her perch, "I'm so sorry." The black-and-white pigeon fluttered onto his forearm, while Becky squawked indignantly.

≈ One Survives ≈

"Hi Becky," Claire said. "We're here to take you home!" She extended her own arm, somewhat warily, but the Rhode Island Red scooted away and flapped from the kitchen table onto the floor.

"Well, come on, then," Jerry said, leading them out. And when he had stepped from the stoop into the snow, Becky flew to his shoulder, grazing Claire's face with her thrashing wings. Then they headed back to the car, Jerry carting Becky on one shoulder and Patty on the other.

They walked more leisurely now, recognizing the time as an opportunity to talk. Jerry was first to mention the topic plaguing Claire's mind. "We're going to have to tell your mother the truth, Claire, of how we met in the woods. Even about your midnight escapade," he said. "Otherwise, how can she trust me as a friend?"

"Must we do it today?"

"No, not today, but soon and together." Then another thought popped into his head. "But you know, we don't have to mention about my birds on the kitchen table." He gave her a quick wink. Claire giggled her consent and skipped ahead, while Jerry slogged along in oversized boots, now with Patty perched atop his head.

The next morning—another clear, brisk day—Claire chose her regular seat in the middle of the bus, but Victor sat in the front. When the bus pulled up to the school, he was the first to scoot off, meeting Billy at curbside. Claire moved quickly down the aisle and off the bus behind Victor.

The school building, an ugly, meandering one-story brown brick with stingy slits for windows, sat a hundred feet from the curb. Dozens of students converged toward its steel doors, but none wanted to enter. They stalled in small groups along the walkway, postponing the inevitable. Claire took cover behind a group of three girls taking pictures of one another with their cell phones. She watched Billy position himself alongside the front door to harass those who entered, while Victor leaned against the building, staring at the sky. Quite unexpectedly, the three girls moved, opening a line of sight between Billy and her.

"Hey, Bird Girl!" Billy hollered from thirty feet away.

Claire jumped as with an electric shock.

"Lose anything lately?" He wore a malevolent grin.

Victor clutched his arm. "Don't call her that!"

Billy ripped loose his arm. "What? She your girlfriend now, Arquetana?"

Claire shouted so that everyone stopped to listen. "I got Sammy back!" The force of her fury startled everyone, especially Billy, whose exposed eye darted among the many watching faces.

"Get a grip," he said, chuckling to act cool.

"No!" she said, charging him. "You get a grip!" and pushed him so hard that he stumbled backward, landing on his bottom. But before he could bounce onto his feet, she was standing over him, shouting, "And don't you dare touch him again!"

Like a flock of noisy starlings, the onlookers responded with chuckles and whistles and timid titters that drove Billy to his feet in a headlong rush to the steel door, behind which he quickly disappeared. Victor smiled at Claire, who was too awash in adrenaline to notice as she marched up the school steps.

Throughout the school day, students who only ever gawked at her now smiled or even said "Hi." And the boy with crooked teeth who sat beside her in computer lab said, "Way to go—you know, this morning, with Billy." But the school day's biggest surprise was at its end, when Victor, smiling as shyly as when they were new friends, strode down the bus aisle and sat beside her.

Victor settled back into his seat, looking somewhat timidly toward Claire. "Way to go today with Billy. Everybody's talking about it."

Claire blushed.

"What did he do to Sammy?"

Her opportunity had finally come to describe Billy's wicked deeds, but something made her hesitate.

"It had to be something awful," he said apologetically.

"He was a jerk, as always," she said. "But I don't want to talk about him. Tell me something about the Mars Mission."

"Tahwach," he said, grinning. "You don't really want to hear about the mission."

She had forgotten her Cochiti name; he had not used it for so long.

"Look at me," he said sweetly. "Why must you always look away?"

With downward, glancing eyes, shielded from view by a thick mantle of snowy lashes, she whispered, "Why won't you tell me your Pueblo name?"

Victor craned his head to look into her eyes, but she pulled away. "Not yet, Tahwach."

18
The Glass Eye

The store vexed Claire. As if overnight, their home had become public property, with people pulling in and out from the patch of gravel in front of the store all day long. And if that weren't enough, sometimes a customer would unknowingly push through the swinging door into their living room!

The only consolation was Jerry. He now arrived by Tucker "taxi" every Friday night with half a dozen pies to sell on Saturday. His guest room sat atop a flight of stairs leading up from the storage area beside the storeroom. This long and narrow space, actually a loft for more storage, perfectly suited Jerry for its privacy and rustic character.

Today, however, was only Tuesday, and though past five thirty, the supper table was not set. Instead, Claire was to serve herself from a pot of vegetable soup atop the cookstove. Within the stove's warmth, on a braided rug in the summer kitchen, she lay with Sammy, brooding about how the store ruined everything. And though her stomach groaned for the simmering soup filling the room with its aroma, she stared obstinately at the inky blackness outside the windows.

Claire hadn't brooded for long when her mother called her into the store to meet someone. At the counter stood a short man with jet-black hair to his shoulders, just like Victor.

"Claire," Louise said, raising her brows high, "this is Victor's father, George Arquetana." Open-mouthed, Claire stood wordless. Before her stood the man who, with Big Red's help, had found her as a lost toddler in the woods, sleeping under an oak tree.

George smiled with kind, dark eyes more solemn than Victor's. "I hear from Victor that you spend lots of time in the woods."

"Yes," Claire said, groping for another word that wouldn't come.

Grinning, he added, "I guess you don't remember me from eight years ago, when you got lost in the woods?"

She shook her head no. George's speech, like Victor's, was almost melodic, rising and falling with uncommon inflection. Claire listened more to its music than its meaning.

"Well, I'm certainly glad you and Victor are friends," he said, turning toward her mother. Then, quite solemnly, he told them that Billy Hollow had been abducted by his father, Clyde, and asked whether either had been in the store recently.

"Victor's Billy?" Claire asked, amazed to learn that a father could kidnap a son.

"Yes," said George. "Victor knew something was wrong when Billy didn't log on to their game." Louise poured a cup of coffee for their guest and invited him to sit at the small table near the checkout counter. "Billy lives with his aunt, but his father is allowed visiting privileges," he said, taking a seat. "He's snatched Billy from school before." He tapped the surface of his coffee with a forefinger.

"Is that coffee okay?" Louise asked.

"It's fine. I was offering some to my grandfather and grandmother spirits, something akin to saying grace before meals."

Claire was fascinated. "Does Victor touch his food before eating, too?" She now sat atop the counter by the register, looking down at them.

"He was raised to," said George, "but whether he does when I'm not watching, I can't say."

"Claire, don't sit on the counter and don't interrupt Mr. Arquetana." She tilted her head toward the swinging door, and Claire slid off the countertop and left the storeroom, inspired to call Victor. She grabbed the phone and hid in the dark stairwell behind the latched door.

Home alone, Victor was eager to talk.

"He's kidnapped Billy before, you know. Took him to West Virginia on a hunting trip, even though Billy's afraid of guns since getting his eye shot out when he was seven—"

"His eye was shot out?"

"You didn't know?"

"How would I know? You never told me!"

"Everybody knows," said Victor. "Why do you think he wears his hair like that? To cover his glass eye."

Billy's solitary eye staring reproachfully filled her mind. How she loathed it, imagining that it sought to reveal the truth of her own eyes.

"Who shot it out?"

"Some kid with a BB gun. Clyde is a fanatic about hunting and can't stand it that Billy's afraid, so he's always forcing him to go along on hunting trips, to get him used to it."

"Have you seen it?" she tried to sound casual. "His glass eye, I mean."

"Sure," Victor boasted. "He's even taken it out for me to hold."

Claire's heart sank. Billy had the courage to reveal an eyeless socket to Victor, yet still she hid her yellow eyes from him. "I hit him in the head with a rock," she said abruptly.

"Billy? When? He never said anything."

"No, his father. I hit his father in the head with a rock because he was trying to shoot Big Red." Claire poured out everything so long held within—from Billy showing her the stuffed red-tail to Billy stealing Sammy. She did not pause in the telling, and Victor could not comment; he could only listen. But in his quiet attention, she felt a comfort slowly releasing her from agitation. Then she turned to the topic of Jerry.

"He's baking pies!" cried Victor in astonishment.

"You wouldn't know him now, honest," said Claire, relieved by the change of topic. The more distant their conversation ranged from Billy, the easier it flowed. And soon they were chatting merrily, renewing all her hopes that Victor would become her best friend.

Next morning, as the bus pulled up to school, Victor leaned across Claire to look out the window for Billy, who was nowhere to be seen. "If he's gone much longer," Victor said, annoyed, "we'll lose our lead to Mars." But the next day, Billy stood curbside, looking expectantly in the passing windows for Victor. Claire had expected to feel sympathy for Billy knowing about his glass eye because she, too, had something to hide. Yet her stomach sank, as it always did, when that solitary eye connected with her own, and she quickly looked away.

"He's back!" Victor crowed, pushing his face past Claire's. "Where've you been?" He shouted through the window, but Billy only pointed to the bus doors, sidestepping in that direction. Victor flew down the aisle toward Billy while Claire stayed seated, awaiting the tide of students to wash through. As the two passed below her open window, she caught an exchange between them.

"I was skeet shooting in Ohio," said Billy. "Practice for duck hunting."

"But we've almost lost our lead," Victor lamented.

"We can make up time." Billy draped an arm over Victor's shoulder. "Don't sweat it."

19
Search for the Snowy Owl

Over the Christmas break, Claire had time to think about all the changes in her life. Most significantly, Jerry was moving into the guest room! Her mother had realized how much she depended upon him. On a Saturday morning before opening the store, she had made him a business proposition: free room and board and a small salary in exchange for a thirty-five-hour work-week. Jerry had nearly dropped his golden-frosted lemon meringue pie.

"Live here?" The idea appeared a puzzle to him. "Every day?"

Her mother hurriedly assured Jerry that she would improve his current room, which had before served as storage space over the back of the store. "I'll put in a nice big window and closet. And that small bathroom at the stair bottom can be for your private use."

Claire watched the sumptuous citrus-smelling pie tilting dangerously in the old man's grasp. She grabbed it. "But Mom, don't the customers use that bathroom?"

"Oh! That's right." She sighed, biting her lower lip in thought. "But it's seldom used," she added earnestly. "And I'll clean it after we close every day."

To this Claire gleefully added, "And you can bake pies in the summer kitchen!"

Jerry looked from one to the other, unable to keep up. Their offer of a new life was miraculous. His eyes began to water but froze with a chilling thought. "My birds," he said as a question and plea.

"Bring them! Bring them, of course!" Neither Claire nor her mother expected what happened next. Jerry sat on a crate behind the pie display case and cried.

The next morning was cold and quiet. Claire lay across her bed staring out to the frozen pond, asleep under a fresh blanket of sparkling snow. First to explore this new terrain were the squirrels, whose meandering tracks suggested a thorough survey. But Claire would have to wait for thicker ice before inviting Victor to go ice skating. Tapping against the windowpane was Narcissus, a flame-red male cardinal. The curious bird frequently visited, seeking the sunflower seeds she scattered over the roof and his reflection in the small panes of her widow.

Tap . . . tap . . . tap-tap . . . tap. "Tell him a-bout us," Narcissus seemed to say, a message hidden within the rhythm of his tapping. Rolling onto her stomach, chin propped upon a folded arm, she watched Narcissus, his crested head bobbing along a span of glass. "What if I did tell him?" she asked. But Narcissus did not want to chat and flew away. With a surge of inspiration, Claire jumped from the bed to search her closet. From the farthest corner on top of the highest shelf, she retrieved a past Christmas present from her great-grandmother in Ireland, a midnight blue hooded sweatshirt with the image of a perfect snowy owl, its feathers dusted with glitter. Except for wearing it to pose in Christmas pictures, Claire had never again passed its fabric over her head, not because she didn't love the snowy owl sweatshirt but because it wouldn't work.

Snowy owls were not native to the woods of central Pennsylvania but to the arctic tundra, where they blended with the landscape to hunt their principal prey, lemmings. Even their winter migration southward took them mostly to Canada and some to upstate New York. How, then, could she expect to see one if she wore the sweatshirt outside? But Claire knew more than before about snowy owls. During winters of scarce food, these large, sleek owls did migrate south into Pennsylvania. And being mostly daytime hunters (diurnal), they might possibly be sighted.

She pushed her head through the sweatshirt and stared into the dresser mirror at herself and the owl. Her naked eyes were the color of the owl's and her hair as white as his feathers. She was going to go out in search of a snowy owl—a somewhat rare sighting. If she found one, she would repeat the performance for Victor to at once tell him her secret and prove her ability. Down the steps she raced, intent on outrunning Sammy to the front door. But wise to her plan, the sheepdog plunged ahead at the curve in the stairwell, almost knocking her down. The racket did not go unnoticed, and her mother intercepted them at the front door.

"Where do you think you're going?" she said.

"Out!"

"Out!" Sammy echoed in a sharp bark.

"I don't think so," her mother said, hands on hips. "Did you forget? We're helping Jerry move stuff in this morning."

"Not now!" Claire cried, knowing the futility of her words, and turned to stomp away.

During the drive to Jerry's town house, they sat silently in the frosty air of irritation until distracted by a silver vintage Jeep parked on the shoulder of the highway, just beneath an overpass. Its occupants, Victor and his father, were climbing out of the vehicle, looking across the road to a steep, graded hillside alongside the bridge.

"Stop!" Claire shrieked, and the car brakes responded. The jolt startled them both.

"Don't EVER do that again!" her mother cried while Claire scrambled to free herself from the seat belt.

"It's Victor," she said, plunging from the car to dart across the road.

Victor and George had turned toward the sound of squealing brakes and now watched as Claire dashed toward them. But Victor ran up to her, pressing a finger against his lips. "It's a snowy owl!" he whispered.

Claire gawked, quickly covering her gaping mouth. "I was just looking for one," she said, words muffled behind her palm.

"What?" But Victor was distracted, dashing off to intercept her mother, just then crossing the highway.

Claire had never seen a snowy owl. This sighting would be an addition to her Life List, a list kept by birders of every bird identified by sight or sound. The image of the owl lay beneath her snow jacket; she need only open it to show Victor. Though she couldn't possibly tell him now of her mystical ability, she could show him the image and explain later. She darted to join the others roadside.

Claire stood reverently, like a devotee at a shrine, watching the placid white owl, who seemed bored by their attention. Huddled within a hollow against a strong wind, the owl watched from high on the hillside with one golden eye, the other closed. Claire's beating heart gave pulse to the owl against her chest, as if the bird existed both on the hillside and within her. She had read enough to know that the owl, completely white, was an adult male. Against the hillside, he appeared as just a patch of snow. But her binocular vision revealed the truth: an arctic predator so heavily feathered as to nearly conceal his bill, toes, and claws. His was a downy armor the wind could ruffle but never penetrate. Into the golden eye of this unfathomable being she stared, searching for insight into his spirit. As before, with Big Red, she felt mesmerized by the owl's pupil. It expanded before her field of vision, a black pool within which she stood poised to dive until yanked back by a tug upon her sleeve. It was Victor.

"Let's go; it's too frigid out here." As bullying winds chased them to their vehicles, Victor triumphantly added, "This time I showed YOU a bird!"

Claire uttered no response but rather opened her jacket to show him the glitter-dusted white owl, committing herself to later reveal the secret held so tightly for so long. With mild interest Victor gazed toward the image that, filling his eyes, pushed up his brows. "You knew about the owl?" he asked, looking for an explanation to the coincidence. "You came out to see it?"

Claire responded wordlessly, shaking her head, "No."

Annoyance began to shade his expression. "So, what then?"

20
Embers and Ash

Before Claire could connect her seat belt, Victor was tapping at the passenger window. "Dad says I can help at Jerry's—if you want." He eagerly opened the back door. Claire was thrilled, certain he came to find out more about her owl sweatshirt. But he quickly scattered this theory when scrunching to the seat edge. "I can't wait to see his place; they say it smells like a chicken coup inside." But Jerry's town house smelled only mildly of chicken and was perfectly empty but for a few packed boxes.

The easy move left Claire and Victor with a free afternoon. Fleeing clouds had buffed a blue diamond sky, and the snow sparkled under a blazing sun. Looking for adventure, they asked Jerry, unpacking baking pans in the summer kitchen, if they could fetch Becky and Patty from the cabin. He politely refused. "They won't stay with you," he explained as they turned dejectedly away. "But you can let them out for air," he said, relenting. "I can't get there for a bit—but NO dog!"

The two flew outside while Sammy barked from within the storeroom. Squinting against the dazzling sun everywhere mirrored in a light fleece of snow, they sprinted across the road. They hurried to outrun the sound of Sammy, barking now from the bay window. Once out of sight, they stopped for breath beneath the oak tree. The frigid air brought rosy blooms to their cheeks and froze their nostril hairs. Even so, Victor pulled back his parka hood. "How far is the cabin?"

"Not far," said Claire, heart pounding from more than exertion. She wanted to tell him her secret before losing resolve. But how to start? She unzipped her jacket to reveal the owl.

🙠 *An Odd Bird* 🙢

The sparkle of her sweatshirt caught his attention. "Hey, you never told me about the owl." He nodded to her shirt front. "How did you know it would be there?"

"I didn't know." She traced a gloved finger over the large fissures of the oak bark.

"Cool coincidence," he said, looking to the fast-flowing creek.

"I don't think it was a coincidence."

"What do you mean?"

"Remember when I told you I was wearing a T-shirt of a red-tail when Big Red found me under the tree?"

He cocked his head in recollection. "Yeah. Your grandmothers gave it to you."

"Yes!" she cried, gaining confidence. "My grandmothers sent me this shirt, too." She opened both sides of her jacket for closer inspection.

Victor squinted against her suggestion. "What are you saying?"

Claire wanted him to make the connection because it might sound less crazy coming from his own mouth. "When I wore a hawk on my shirt, I saw a hawk; when I wore an owl, I saw an owl."

Victor laughed. "Now you're being funny."

She could tell he thought it a game. She stepped on a high tree root and posed a question. "Once might be a coincidence, but twice?"

Victor played along. "Maybe your grandmothers can do magic, like fairy godmothers. Maybe they put charms on those shirts."

"That's what I thought!" She turned quickly back to him, slipping off the root. "At least when I was younger." She hoped he would pursue the discussion, but instead he darted down the rocky hillside toward the fast-flowing creek.

The trip to the cabin was easy and quick now that she knew the way. How it had remained hidden from her for so long remained a mystery. Claire prided herself as a scout and this far-reaching forest her frontier. Though she and Sammy generally followed regular routes, she had thoroughly surveyed the borders of her "kingdom"; at least she had thought so.

With a perfect frosting of rooftop snow, the cabin looked lovely, not at all like the dried-out husk of her memory. The open-air windows were shuttered on sagging hinges to keep out the cold and predators. Anxious to free the prisoners within, Claire yanked open the door and the birds blasted out. "You poor babies," cried Claire, delighted with their deliverance. Becky wildly thrashed the frigid air yet sank to the ground while Patty flew into a shrubby pine tree, dusting the air with freshly fallen snow.

"I wonder if she remembers me," said Victor, approaching the Rhode Island Red, who skittered away.

"Don't scare them off," chided Claire.

Victor bounded into the cabin. "It stinks in here. Should we open these shutters?"

"I guess." She stepped through the doorsill as he did so. From the floor she collected soiled newspapers spread in the corner beneath roosts for the birds, a wooden cubbyhole for the pigeon, and a large open drawer with straw for Becky. Both were set atop a squat cupboard adjacent to a frozen bowl of water and tin platter of chicken feed. Otherwise, the cabin held a sleeping cot, small wooden table with chair, a utility table with a metal coffeepot, iron skillet, and some silverware, a box of matches, a big pile of firewood lined against the opposite

An Odd Bird

wall, and a stack of newspapers from which Claire retrieved fresh catch-paper for beneath the roosts.

With an armful of fouled newspapers, she emerged from the cabin to discover Henry, the distinguished ring-necked pheasant, strutting behind the plump chicken beyond the fire ring. Standing at the threshold behind her, his warm breath rising in the air, Victor whispered, "Jerry has a pheasant, too?"

"No, he's wild, but he likes Becky."

They watched the unlikely couple disappear behind a dense thicket of autumn olive bushes crowding the outhouse. Victor dropped from the doorsill behind Claire, who dumped the newspapers in the center of the fire ring. Then she turned to him, eyes ablaze. "Let's start a fire!" Hurriedly they constructed a lopsided teepee of tinder and wood and gratefully crowded the sprouting orange-yellow flames. After a while Victor carelessly dumped a heavy log onto the burning scaffold, sending a spray of embers and ash into the air.

"Ah!" Claire jumped up, covering her left eye. "I got something in my eye!"

"I'm sorry!" he cried, crowding her to see the injury, but she angrily turned away.

"It's really big," she said, blinking to dislodge the debris but recoiling from his every effort to assist her. Twisting away, she slipped in the snow and fell. "Ow!" she shrieked in annoyance more than pain. Victor was trying to help her up when Jerry arrived, Becky perched upon his shoulder. He raced to assist them.

"She's got something in her eye," Victor said. "She won't let me see."

Now Claire had two nosey bodies to fend off, each grabbing an arm to pull her up while Becky clucked with agitation. Standing, she shook free her arms, left eye screwed shut. For a moment they all vented hot breath into the air. Jerry was first to speak. "You'll have to take out your lenses."

Clasping a hand over the injured eye, Claire opened the other in dismay.

"You wear lenses?" Victor asked, merely curious, but she didn't answer, good eye popping with entreaty toward the old man.

"Come here," he said, waving her in with one hand and excluding Victor with the other. "Let me see."

"He doesn't know," she whispered while Jerry's calloused fingers pried open her sore eye. Becky's fat feathered red breast loomed large before her upturned face.

"It doesn't matter," he said. "The lens has to come out."

Claire scuttled backward, urgently blinking.

"It's lodged right under the lens, at the edge, and it'll scratch your eye, if it hasn't already."

Though standing in the open, Claire felt cornered. The debris became more painful beneath her lid with each blink; its sharp edge like a razor. Could she remove the lens and then reinsert it before Victor could see? "Okay." She darted into the cabin, shouting, "Everybody stay out!"

With the lens came the debris, a speck so small she could hardly see it. Her eye, however, was too sore to put the lens back in, yet even as she moaned aloud, a revelation hit—she didn't need to! Her eye was sore; she needed only to keep it shut. From the cabin she emerged visibly relieved, offering the speck on her fingertip for inspection.

21
Exposed

Jerry had brought a welcome surprise, a thermos of hot chocolate and three tin cups. To enjoy this treat, they arranged three tree stumps in a huddle before the blazing fire. The heat from without and now within melted prior tensions as they relaxed into conversation. Victor wanted to know how Jerry had tamed the wild pheasant.

"I didn't tame her," he said, as if charged with a crime.

"But wild pheasants won't—"

"I told you," Claire said, interrupting. "He visits Becky."

But Jerry had another explanation. "Birds just like me."

Claire's eyes widely opened. "They do?" She cupped a hand to her injured one.

"Some do," he said, offering his whiskered cheek to Becky for an affectionate peck. "I first noticed as a young boy when this huge grayish bird flew into our pond. I thought he didn't see me 'cause I sat under a willow. He waded on these long stick legs into the water. I was fascinated. His neck was so long that it curled in on itself and he had a long, stout bill, dagger-like."

"A great blue," said Claire, demonstrating expertise.

"Yes, but to a boy of six, this was some magical critter. Mind you, I thought I was fishing with a string on a stick. So there I sat, eyes ogling this fancy bird with fringes on its feathers and wispy black head plumes." He lifted Becky from his shoulder to gently deposit onto the ground. "I watched him stalk the shallows, neck extended, eyes surveying the water

❧ Exposed ❦

and then——BAM!" His palms smacked together. "He grabs a bluegill and swallows it whole."

Nodding, Claire said, "Herons fish at our pond, too."

Jerry's hazel eyes glinted with challenge. "But no blue ever came high-stepping right up to you, I bet."

"He didn't!" she cried.

"Oh, yes he did, and more besides." His companions raptly attending, Jerry explained how the great blue heron had jumped from the pond to stand alongside him, as if a fishing buddy. More incredibly, he returned throughout that summer, each time keeping company and even sharing fish with him. This story seemed too incredible to believe. Claire and Victor shook their heads, chuckling against it, which so vexed Jerry that he stood and called for his birds. "We're leaving," he said, as Patty flew to his shoulder and Becky bounced into his hands. "Be sure to douse the fire with water!" He pointed to a barrel beneath the cabin eaves.

Speechless with guilt, the two watched as Jerry tramped away, birds swaying to his gait, hot breath rising as a cloud into the cold air. "And don't be long!" They wanted to chase after him, to apologize, but had to douse the fire and so called out their regrets. "We didn't mean it!" cried Claire. "We're sorry!" cried Victor. In response, Jerry raised a hand but did not look back. When he was out of sight, they consoled one another.

"Boy, he's touchy," said Victor, kicking a loose ember back into the fire.

"He really is," said Claire.

"I thought he was just having fun, playing a game, like you, earlier, with the magic bird shirts."

"But it wasn't a game!"

These words popped of their own accord from Claire's mouth, over which she slapped a hand. Her eyes, one golden and the other blue-gray, filled with astonishment. In Victor's squinting gaze, she saw another error and quickly hid her one amber eye behind her free hand.

He attempted to pry this hand from her eye. "Let me see!"

In a burst a futility, she pushed him away. "Fine!" she cried. "Look all you want." And into his face she pushed her own.

Victor's eyes bounced between hers, looking first at the watering golden and then at the blue. Finally, with a bit of a whine, he said, "I don't understand."

She snorted a sigh. "I wear blue-tinted contacts to conceal my real eye color." She poked a finger toward her injured eye. "It's bad enough I have white hair and skin. Can you imagine if I went to school with yellow eyes?"

"It's not yellow," he said, "but . . . honey-colored. Take out the other one."

After some struggle to remove gloves, with cold hands Claire manage to extract the other lens. Sitting as close as possible to the fire, he inspected her eyes, mesmerized. His steady gaze snapped with a sudden thought. "Hey, let me see your owl shirt again."

She urgently unzipped her parka, buried cold hands into its pockets, and flung open her jacket front.

"How cool! You've the same eye color as the owl!" His dark brown eyes, lit with discovery, sought her snowy hair beneath the parka hood. She pushed it back, knowing exactly what he would say: "Tahwach, you look like a snowy owl." He meant it as a sincere compliment, but Claire responded with a cheerless smile. She understood the bigger truth: other people didn't look like owls.

Seeing his mistake, Victor tried to fix it. "I mean—you're beautiful!"

Claire looked away, tears blurring her vision. "You're just saying that." She popped up the hood and dug for her gloves.

"I mean it," he said, chasing her face, but she kept twisting away. "And now I understand."

She stopped, face averted. "Understand what?"

"About the birds."

"What about them?"

"That they come to you, but I need to see for myself." He held up his hand to block any complaint. "NOT because I don't believe you, but because I need to study the situation."

Claire was happy. She finally had a friend with whom to investigate her life's biggest mystery. Yet she couldn't help but point out the obvious. "Today should count," she said, glancing to the snowy owl on her chest before zipping up the parka, fingertips numb with cold.

"Nah. I found that one." He strode toward a rubber bucket that sat beside the water barrel. "Let's douse the fire and get back."

22
A Chickadee Cheats Death

The next morning, on New Year's Day, Claire fretted over what bird to select for her outing with Victor. Sitting on the bed, she sifted through a high stack of bird cards while Sammy watched from bedside, wooly head propped atop the mattress. Let's go, go, go! he kept saying with wagging tail and begging eyes that peeked through wooly bangs. But she kept replying, "Just wait!" until finally, in defeat, he slumped to the rug.

Selecting a bird wasn't simple. In winter, there were fewer from which to choose; only a few dozen hardy species lived year-round in Pennsylvania. Other, nonresident birds flew south as their food sources became scarce. This mass departure always left Claire feeling wistful as the chatter and song of woodland birds faded into silence. Yet winter also promised the arrival of some northern breeding birds for whom Pennsylvania was "south." Some of these, who bred in Canada and Alaska, included the dark-eyed junco, the American tree sparrow, and the northern shrike. And it was this last, a predatory songbird, that she selected.

The shrike fed on smaller birds and had a ghoulish habit of impaling his victims upon thorns, barbed wire, or other sharp spurs. Such odd behavior would surely intrigue Victor. Having no shirt image of this chunky gray-and-black bird, Claire took as her lure the identification card. Pressing it against her heart, she jumped from bed, to Sammy's great relief, and together they dashed down the winding stairs.

Fighting to poke an arm through the sleeve of her brown-fleece jacket, Claire pushed out the front door as Victor climbed

A Chickadee Cheats Death

the porch stoop, his father waving from the Jeep as he pulled away. "Sammy, down!" she cried as the sheepdog, in delirious greeting, dove into his chest.

"I don't mind," said Victor, laughing, as he gripped the swaggering dog in an affectionate hug.

All plunged into the day under a low, gray sky muffling the sun. Gone was the burning cold. Sammy bounded over the slick yet thawing snow path that his companions navigated less well. For better footing, Claire cut across the open snow, sloping down to the woodland, where within its naked branches she saw agitated activity. She stopped to focus as Victor, stepping alongside, followed her gaze. Two birds appeared to be playing, one chasing the other about the limbs of several trees. But one bird was much bigger than the other. Both Claire and Victor could identify the smaller a bird, a black-capped chickadee, but neither could make out the larger one. In a nonstop game of "tag," this bigger bird, about the size of a robin, followed the chickadee's maneuvers—up, down, and sideways through the branches.

"I don't think they're playing," said Victor. "That big one is trying to catch the chickadee."

Victor was right! Claire could now see the flight of the chickadee as fitful, not playful. And with each new launch from branch to branch, the small bird barely escaped his pursuer.

"He's getting tired," said Victor grimly.

"We'll scare him off!" cried Claire as she jogged toward the tree line but quickly slipped and fell onto her bottom. Victor stopped to help, but she smacked away his hand. "The chickadee!" she cried, urging him onward. Turning, he lunged ahead, hollering as he ran to distract the predator. The tactic worked, for the chunky bird flew opposite the chickadee that, with feeble effort, flew into open air. Seeing his vulnerable prey, the killer songbird gave chase despite the hazard of humans. Victor shrieked alarm as Claire, stumbling to her feet, saw the small black-capped and bibbed bird thrashing through the air toward her. His furious flight suddenly slackened, as if to slow his motion, wings folding and unfolding, down and up, down and up. Somehow snared by time, the chickadee made no forward progress. Above and behind, the northern shrike, seen now by Claire, hung menacingly in space. Time resumed with an eye blink and a flash of white wing; the chickadee had perched upon her shoulder! She ducked as the shrike, about to collide with her head, pulled upward. Where the chickadee had perched, Claire saw empty space: the shrike had taken him!

She groaned as Victor jogged up to her. "He got the chickadee," she said, head bent in defeat.

"He didn't; he's clutching your collar."

Claire gasped. Tilting his cheek, she could feel his soft form against her neck but still could not see him. "What's he doing?"

"Just hanging there." Victor scanned the sky for the attacker. "That predator is probably still around, waiting."

"It was a northern shrike," said Claire meaningfully, but Victor couldn't understand; she hadn't yet told him of her selection, of the identification card.

"Well, that shrike"—he emphasized the word for her benefit—"is still around." He turned to scan the tree line from which he had flown. "Maybe he won't try for the chickadee if we take him back to your yard."

As he spoke, Claire retrieved the card from her deep zipper pocket and extended it to him. "Look." While he gazed at the card, she crunched her shoulder to cuddle the tiny bird against her cheek. "I can't believe this chickadee flew right to me," she said in a soft, cooing voice.

❧ A Chickadee Cheats Death ☙

Victor looked up from the image of the northern shrike and into the amber eyes hidden behind their tinted lenses. "I can," he said with the conviction of a convert. "I definitely can."

23
Matter of Mind

Claire sat with Victor beneath the spruce tree beside the pond. Here they had come, shouldering their backpacks, from the steps of the school bus. Sammy happily escorted them until realizing their intention to sit on the bench. Against this plan, he pounced playfully about, head low, hind end high, tail wagging. But Claire paid him no mind, digging within her pack for a notebook and pen. Nor did his sharp bark arouse them, so he dashed alone down the sloping bank behind them.

"So where should we start?" said Claire, propping the notepad upon her thigh. After their encounter with the chickadee and the shrike, she had engaged Victor as coinvestigator into the mystery of her skills. They sat outside for privacy, for the temperature was well above freezing. Not a patch of snow remained over the gray-green grass, and slush covered the frozen pond. Victor used his parka as a cushion on the hard bench. The sweet, chill air was refreshing after a long day at school.

"Let's eliminate explanations that don't make sense."

"Good." Claire readied her pen.

"Your bird shirts can't be the cause, because you weren't wearing one yesterday."

Claire sighed. "True . . . I didn't wear one yesterday, but typically I see birds that I wear."

"*Typically* doesn't count," he said officiously. "Yesterday you had an ID card; maybe you just need a bird's image on your person."

Henry flashed to mind. "No," she said decisively. "I saw the ring-necked pheasant without a shirt or an ID card."

Victor stood. "But you carried a mental image of the pheasant, right?"

Claire jumped from the bench. "Yes!" She bounced with enthusiasm. "Victor, could it be that simple?"

Satisfaction gleamed in his dark eyes. "I think so." He scratched his scalp to stir up new thoughts. "Still . . . it only explains what you do—not how it works or even why it works. I mean what do birds want with you?"

"It's a start!" she shouted into the hazy sky between upstretched arms. Dropping them abruptly, she turned to Victor. "I knew you could help; I knew it."

Victor shook his head, trying not to smile so widely. "We still need to figure out how it works." He sat again on the bench. With Claire settled beside him, he continued, "Maybe you broadcast those mental images, and the birds who recognize themselves answer the 'call.' Like a person who responds when his or her name is called."

Claire grinned with skepticism. "You mean telepathically."

"Yeah." Victor shrugged. "I think lots of animals communicate that way."

She giggled at the idea. "You're saying that birds are reading my mind—a person's mind? Don't you think that's far-fetched?"

"No more than birds seeking you out when you want them to."

She sank back onto the bench to think about this.

"It's not like they know the English language," he said. "They just recognize themselves—their species—in your mind."

Claire exhaled loudly, not ready to concede.

❧ An Odd Bird ❦

"But then again"—Victor chuckled—"maybe they do know English. Jerry seems to think so, the way he talks to his birds."

Mention of Jerry brought to mind another theory, one Claire had been wrestling over for some time. "About Jerry," she said, twisting to put her face near his ear, "something's really strange about him."

Victor, expecting some serious confidence, thought the comment comical and laughed.

"No, I'm serious," she said, scolding him. "I think he's here purposely, with some kind of plan."

Victor could not stop laughing. He stood to compose himself, wiping a tear from his eye. "He's been weird from the start, and you're just now noticing?"

"No, no! It's something more than that," she said. "Sit down and listen." Claire explained her sense that Jerry possessed unusual abilities with birds, much like herself, but also different. She felt that every encounter, from their first, had been arranged and that he orchestrated situations to produce particular results. To start, she had not seen things this way. Her first encounter with him (hidden beneath low-lying hemlock branches) was mere coincidence, or so she had believed. Likewise, she thought that they had caused the second encounter by chasing him through the woods. But what if he actually had led them? And how likely could it be that Jerry should find her, after midnight, lost in the woods? She hurriedly recounted all this as background, intending to emphasize more recent events. However, Victor had now become the skeptic.

"I agree that he bonds with birds—especially if you believe his stories." A roll of eyes suggested he might not. "I mean, really, a great blue heron fished with him all summer?"

"That's my point: Jerry's not 'normal.' I think he might be . . . I don't know . . . a wizard or something."

Victor's response was an amused expression that instantly infuriated her. "You're much more fun than Billy," he said, grabbing her hand as he stood. "Let's go check out the wizard's birds. I'm getting cold sitting here."

Claire's mother had purchased a new chicken coop for Jerry's birds. Roomy and new, the house had both a transom window for Patty and a fenced-in run for Becky. It sat across from the pond at the base of the hill, populated by wild cherry trees. Both birds, pecking at the soggy ground, looked up and beyond them as they approached. Claire turned toward the house. "That's right. It's time for Jerry's outing with the birds. I bet they're looking for him."

Victor stepped spritely onto the hillside above the house. "Quick—come here!" he called, ducking below the coop roofline. Claire saw what he was up to.

"That's not going to work," she said, climbing up beside him. "He's probably seen us already."

He pulled her down by the hand. "Let's see."

Victor crouched close against the outside wall, with Claire a bit higher beside him. Whispering together, they waited for Jerry. When Sammy began barking, Claire cried, "Oh, no," he'll blow our cover!"

"Maybe not," said Victor. "I think he's barking at the back door." He peeked over the roof to catch a glimpse. "Yes! Sammy's going in and Jerry's coming out." That meant they had a couple of minutes before he would reach the coop.

"This is stupid," whispered Claire, moving to face Victor against the wall. "We can't see anything."

"We might hear something." He put a finger to his lips.

Her face so close to his, Claire felt like laughing and clutched her mouth. His wide-eyed reprimand made things only worse, and she began to giggle. But hearing Jerry at the screened run, she held her breath until the birds fluttered to the opening gate.

"Becky, my dear," said Jerry, "what did you hear from Henry? You still haven't said."

The snoopers gawked at one another. The sound of hard-flapping wings meant Becky was flying to his shoulder.

He continued, "Come on, Patty. We haven't all day, and I've an errand for you."

Claire and Victor waited for three full minutes before venturing a peek. Jerry was, as they imagined, already far down the path heading opposite the house. This path ran parallel to the base of the hill for about a thousand feet to its flank, where it wound up to an expansive pasture. Popping from their hiding place, they dashed back to the house, eager to huddle in the winding stairwell for a secret council. Safe from prying ears, they sat behind the closed door of the curving stairwell discussing the oddity of what they had heard. "People talk to their pets all the time," said Victor, "but not like that. It was like he was expecting Becky to provide a report."

Claire nodded eagerly. "I know; I know. There are only two—no, maybe three—explanations: one, he's crazy; two, he actually communicates with his birds; and three, he knew we were there and was teasing us. Which do you think?"

Victor considered the options and made a quick decision: "I take all three."

24
Wizard or What?

The next day after school, Jerry and Claire walked to his cabin to retrieve Patty. She had flown from the backyard over the woodland to the cabin that she still saw as "home." To retrieve the pigeon, the two bird lovers had a wonderful excuse for a walk. Claire, however, suspected that Jerry had orchestrated the event, for the day prior he had mentioned to Patty an "errand." What if the errand was that she should purposefully fly off to the cabin?

"It's lucky we've an opportunity to talk," Jerry said as they crossed the road, trailing far behind Sammy.

Ah-ha! Claire thought. He did arrange this outing! As if to check her wild imaginings, he stopped and looked directly to her. Under his earnest gaze, she lowered her veiled eyes, though he knew their true color. "You see," he said, "I've a confession to make." The word "confession" made her uncomfortable, for she had her own: spying on him.

"We'd better catch up with Sammy first," she said, darting over the path. "He's already out of sight." To keep distant was too easy, for the old man moved at a plodding pace. She rooted herself beside the creek, while Sammy waded into his favorite, deep water hole. From the massive oak tree, clinging still to half its leaves, Jerry called down to her: "Come up here for a bit!" Taking the suggestion to heart, Sammy surged from the creek, water rolling from his wooly fur, and charged the incline. Claire meekly followed. As she reached the tree, Jerry was lowering himself onto one of its roots, as thick as an elephant's leg. "Sit." He nodded toward a similar but smaller perch.

☙ *An Odd Bird* ☙

Without preliminaries, he said, "About my confession: I'm not what I seem."

"What do you seem?" Claire said.

"I seem like a crazy old man who used to haunt the woods." He stopped to gaze up into the oak, which, in response, shed a few caressing leaves upon him. "I miss it."

Claire felt sympathy. "But you don't have to stop. The woods are right here, and here we are—right now!"

"You're right; I'm being overly sentimental. Old men get that way."

Sitting beneath the oak, his hair now longer since first cut, Jerry reminded her more of the wild man she found beneath the hemlock tree. He pushed aside a frizzy lock fallen over his forehead. "You see, the woods mean a lot to me, just like to you. It's up to people like us to protect them and their residents."

"You mean the birds and animals?"

"Yes. Birds and animals and insects and plants—all that live."

Sammy, dripping wet and dodging about, had expected something more than a "sit about" under a tree; he headed back toward the creek.

Claire pressed him on his original point. "But if you're not who you seem, who are you?"

With satisfaction, he said, "I am a self-appointed guardian of the woods."

Claire had expected something more decisive. To her, the words "self-appointed" and "guardian" added up to "crazy old man." She could muster no more enthusiasm than, "Oh."

Seeing her disappointment, Jerry offered something more enticing. "Mother Earth takes note of her devotees, Claire. She offers them insights into nature unknown to but few people, such as shamans, yogis, druids, and—"

"And wizards?" Claire asked, eyes widening.

Jerry smiled. "Labels aren't important."

Jumping upward, she said excitedly, "I knew it!" Dropping to her haunches, she nearly fell over. "Will you teach me?"

Jerry hoisted himself upward and away. "You're already being taught," he said, too casually for the enormity of the moment. "The birds are your teachers."

"The birds?"

"Of course. The more birds draw you in, the more you understand them. And understanding birds helps you to understand trees, which helps you to understand squirrels, porcupines, bears, and everyone else dependent on a tree."

Claire was seeking more than an ecology lesson, and she objected to his observation: "You think the birds draw me in?" She chased after his fast-moving figure, amazed at his sudden agility. How could she correct him? How could she tell him that the birds came to her? He appeared entirely inattentive. Arms outstretched for balance, he leaped lightly over the crossing stones of the creek. Jumping onto the bank, he inhaled the unseasonably warm air, and his pleasant expression faded. Suddenly stern, he turned to her. "A hailstorm is coming—quickly. I've time only to get Patty and back again, so get your dog and get home now."

25
Sky Dancing

When not working in the store, Jerry became a mobile roost to Becky and Patty, "airing" his girls outdoors many times a day, regardless of the cold, urging them from his shoulder to flap or fly, as needed. At other times he sat outside the back door, tucked into a corner. There, protected from the wind, he smoked his pipe. Roosting near his neck for warmth, veiled in a smoky gray haze, his feathered companions lent the old man a mythic look, like the wizard Merlin of the King Arthur legend.

A long three weeks and two snowstorms passed before Claire and he could again venture together into the woodland, their destination the rocky outcrop. It was an unseasonably warm day, with temperatures in the low fifties. The afternoon sun softened a crusty snow pack, two inches deep, yet islands of emerald moss suggested greener days to come. At the outcrop, Jerry took his seat on the boulder while Claire scooted to the edge, to dangle her long legs. Quietly they bathed in the blue sky until Jerry raised binoculars to his eyes.

"Guess who brought home a friend?"

"Where?" Claire followed the line of his rising arm. Without having to ask, she knew that he meant Big Red. No sooner had she locked on two distant specks than one plunged from view, as if yanked from below. "Wait!" she yelled. "One's falling!" Then the other fell. Frantically she sought them with her own eyes. "Jerry, what's happening?"

Jerry lowered his binoculars, cupping his eyes to locate the two hawks hurtling downward through the sky.

"Anytime now, Big Red . . . anytime," he muttered.

"What?" Claire didn't understand his meaning or why the hawks were falling from the sky.

"There!" he shouted triumphantly, pointing. The diving figures pulled away and upward, like planes in an aeronautic display, and then flew alongside one another. "There!" Jerry yelled. "At four o'clock and heading this way." They snapped binoculars to their eyes. "Do you see them," he asked, "flying side by side?"

"Yes, yes—no! Wait . . ."

Together the hawks pulled upward, once again out of view. "They're going to dive again," Jerry said breathlessly. "Wait for it . . . wait for it—now!"

One plunged, rolling like a plane caught in a spiral descent. The other dove, like a skydiver, directly to its mate. With one above, the other below, they locked talons, spinning together in a free fall through the blue expanse.

"Oh, my heavens!" Claire cupped her mouth. For long seconds the pair fell, locked in life and potential death, pledging themselves in the courtship dance of red-tails. For these same seconds, Claire did not breathe. When, finally, the hawks split apart, she gulped for air.

26
Foiled Abduction

On Monday morning Claire boarded the bus, bursting to tell Victor of Big Red's new mate and courtship dance. Though it was dreary and cold outside and the bus inside smelled of soggy vinyl, all was beautiful in Claire's world. A person could go her entire life without witnessing a red-tail's courtship, and she couldn't wait to tell Victor. But his disposition matched the day outside. Half asleep, he groggily slumped into the seat beside her, saying with a sigh, "I was up most the night with the mission."

Her resentment growing, Claire watched him sink farther into the seat and pull a cap over his eyes. "You can't sleep. I've got something important to tell you!"

But Victor simply grunted with annoyance. "I don't want to hear another Jerry story," he said, pulling his cap lower. "Let me nap."

Claire kicked the back of the seat in front of her. "You're so stupid, wasting your life on that stupid game."

Victor grunted and tugged his cap back over his eyes.

During lunchtime, Claire sat outside alone, atop her book bag and under a locust tree. The grass, though wet and matted from successive snow blankets, looked vibrantly green and the sky blissfully blue. Other classmates sat on wide cement stairs below Victor and Billy, who sat atop concrete balustrades flanking the entry. Identical in posture, they sat on either side, legs extended, ankles crossed, and eyes closed to soak in the sun. They were energizing themselves for the hours ahead and the long-awaited Mars landing.

ཉ Foiled Abduction ༀ

As lunchtime drew to a close, noisy, jostling students filed between the two, who remained as if sleeping. Claire hoped to slip unnoticed between them until the sound of squealing tires ripped the air, alerting them to the red pickup turning the intersection and gunning toward the school.

"Oh, no," Billy said. "My father."

Legs scrambling beneath him, Victor scooted from the balustrade. "Don't let him take you!" he cried, pulling at Billy, who seemed inert. "We have to land tomorrow."

Standing between them, Claire gasped as the truck jumped the curb, the driver reining it back. Lunging to a stop, the rusting hulk farted a blast of exhaust.

"Billy, get inside!" Victor pulled him by the legs.

Yet as Billy began to slide from the balustrade, his father stumbled over the curb. "Wait right there, boy!" he ordered.

Billy froze. Clyde Hollow looked deranged, his pale, whiskered face contorted.

Claire froze. "Victor, get help!" she said, without looking back. "Do you hear me? Get help!"

Victor looked at Billy and then to the heavy steel doors closed behind him. Clyde Hollow headed toward them like a drugged bull but suddenly stopped. On unsteady legs, he wavered for an instant, staring at Claire.

"You're the girl that hit me with a rock," he said, pointing at her with a heavy arm.

"Victor, get help!" Claire said, more loudly this time, stepping onto the lawn.

"What?" Billy said, as if waking from a nap. "What's he talking about?" he said to Claire, moving alongside her.

Clyde grimaced. "Shut up, Billy, and get in the truck."

"Your father," Claire said, looking not at Billy but his father, "was about to shoot Big Red, so I—"

◈ *An Odd Bird* ◈

"Shut up!" Clyde roared.

Clutching the entrance door handle, Victor yanked it open and scurried inside.

"I'm not telling you again, Billy—Git in the truck."

Billy hesitated an instant before taking a step.

Claire grabbed his arm. "You can't go; he's drunk."

Billy shoved her with his shoulder so hard that she stumbled backward. "Don't ever touch me," he said, looking back, his solitary eye filled with panic.

Claire darted toward the curb. Billy and Clyde watched, thinking she meant to flee, not understanding why she peered into the truck's passenger window. "Yes!" She darted around the front of the truck to the driver's side.

Clyde staggered toward the curb. "What are you doing?!" he yelled, beginning to understand.

Pulling open the driver's side door, she grabbed the ignition key. "You can both get in the truck," she said triumphantly, holding the key over her head like a trophy, "because it's not going anywhere!" And she skipped backward across to the street's opposite curb.

Clyde growled, his face flushing brick red. He sprang forward, collapsing on tangled feet.

Billy ran to his father, lying face down on the wet grass. "Look what you've done!" he screamed, bending down to help his father up.

"Get away!" Clyde shouted, pushing himself up as the front doors of the school sprang open. Spilling out onto the steps were the principal, the school security guard, and Victor.

27
Hallway Hustle

Neither Victor nor Billy attended school on the first day of spring. To anyone who asked, Anthony said with a wink, "They both got 'fevers.'"

Claire hoped that with a successful Mars landing, Victor's "fever" would finally break, and he would spend more time with her. She chose to ignore that the mission didn't end with the landing, for he and Billy must then construct an outpost and await the arrival of other mission members who, with them, would constitute the first colonizers of Mars.

The following day was cold and bleak. Claire sat against the bus window, anxious for news of the landing. At the stop before Victor's, Anthony and Bo boarded, plopping into the seat ahead. "He won't be in today," Anthony said in a quiet voice.

"What?"

"Human error; they burned up entering the Martian atmosphere."

This news was so significant that even Bo, typically tuned only to his music, added an insight: "I think Billy intentionally sabotaged the mission. There's no other explanation."

Claire hadn't conceived of a failed mission, so she didn't know what to say or even think. To stress the situation's enormity, Anthony reviewed the essentials: for three and a half years Victor had prepared for the event, from his earliest flight training in a glider. He and Billy were to have been the first Flight Fever gamers on Mars. And now Victor was finished—dead to the game.

❧ An Odd Bird ❧

"Dead to the game," Claire said aloud, these words alone penetrating the fog of her thoughts.

The bus stopped at Victor's house, idled for a moment, and then pulled away. Anthony, Bo, and Claire all stared mournfully at the place where he would have stood. Ideas began to shape in Claire's mind. Without the mission, Victor would be free of the computer . . . free to go outside . . . free to be with her!

But much to Claire's dismay, Victor didn't attend school on Thursday or Friday. Nor did Billy. But on Monday, Billy kicked open the heavy steel door into the lobby, sending students darting right and left down the main hallway. Claire, too, scurried for cover into the first empty classroom, standing against the wall beside the open door. Entering this hallway from a basement stairwell came Lloyd Blunt, a skinny kid with straggly brown hair, known to be somewhat indifferent to his surroundings.

"Hey, Billy, where've you been?" he asked without interest.

Billy chose to reserve his fury for someone other than Lloyd—the "brain dead," as he called him. "Not at home, like Victor, crying with my mamma," he said, passing the classroom where Claire hid.

Claire's fear was overcome by her fury. She ran out into the hallway. "How can you say that about your friend?!"

Billy stopped and stood motionless. Claire swallowed air. Only a few feet separated them. She could see him blowing air with his lower lip as he turned toward her.

"Victor was never my friend," he spat.

"You're right. Who would want to be friends with you?"

Billy's solitary eye popped. He lunged forward, plowing into her chest, knocking her to the glossy tiled floor, where they both skidded to a stop, Claire on her back, Billy splayed on top, his arms straddling her head. Faces inches apart, they stared at one another in alarm. Hanging free of his glass eye was the curtain of hair kept perpetually in place. This same hair now grazed her forehead, forming a tent within which their eyes locked.

"Get off me!" Claire cried.

Pushing himself upward, Billy was yanked from behind by the school security guard.

"Hey!" Billy squealed, swinging his arms against the force plucking him from the ground.

Claire still lay on the floor, breathless, staring up into the powdered, fleshy face of the principal, Ms. Shay. Claire closed her eyes, inhaling the principal's lilac perfume and listening to Billy's protests as the husky guard pulled him down the hallway. "What about me?!" he was screaming. "What about me?!"

"We're going to tend to you, boy," she could hear the guard saying. "Don't you worry about that."

Claire's only injury was a stiff neck and a small bump on the back of her head. Billy, however, didn't fare as well. During the fall, he jammed his left knee and right elbow; and worse, he was immediately suspended for the rest of the week. On the morning of his return, neither Claire nor Victor was prepared to see him standing curbside at school, awaiting the bus and Victor.

"Why's he waiting on me?" Victor said with words as hard as his expression. Only then did Claire realize how much he resented Billy for the failed Mars Mission. Stepping from the bus into a drizzle of rain, she saw Billy's hopeful expression fade. And she felt sorry for him.

◈ *An Odd Bird* ◈

If the school conflict counselor thought that saving Billy from expulsion would earn his good behavior, she was wrong. His mood was darker and more dangerous than ever, and everyone scattered on his approach. Wherever he went, an empty area formed around him. During lunch break, Victor stared savagely at him, but Billy appeared to enjoy the attention, strutting past Victor, as if some admiring fan.

On the bus home, Victor relayed to Claire this and more. "I avoided him in the cafeteria, but he kept walking past me to the vending machines, at least three times! He was trying to irritate me. Finally I said, 'You're such a loser.' Well, he stopped, looked at the floor, and shook his head. I said it again, but he still didn't look at me, just kept shaking his head." Victor paused to drop his own head in apparent regret. "Then I shouted, 'What's wrong with you?' because something was wrong. And before long, Ms. Li swooped in and took him off to the nurse's office; at least somebody said so." Again, Victor paused before concluding. "It serves him right for being such a louse." But his sad brown eyes said something different. And Claire hoped, for his sake, that Billy would be back to school the next day. And to their relief, Billy did return, though he kept quietly to himself.

28
Dangerous Drunk

Throughout the week Claire and Victor planned to visit the outcrop, and Saturday finally arrived with crisp, delicious air and a tangy blue sky. Jerry couldn't go because it was pie-sale Saturday but asked them to pick up Patty who, yet again, had flown "home" to his cabin. The two agreed, delighted to invest their daytime fun with an official duty, hoisting daypacks stuffed with food and drink onto their backs.

Sammy ignored Claire's decision to leave him behind, nearly knocking over Helen Whiner to dash through the opening store door. But no sooner had he bounded up to them than the sheepdog took off again, chasing after the scent of some deer.

They forged a plan to sneak up on the Fist and Finger, wading quietly through the tangle of mountain laurel leading to these overlooks. Then, from behind a thin stand of white pine, they aimed their binoculars to the Finger and its alcove containing the hawks' nest. Both gasped with the image filling their views: Big Red sitting upon the nest and her smaller mate poised at the ledge, about to take flight. "She must have eggs!" cried Claire as the male plunged into the buoyant sky.

"We need a name for him," Victor said, his binoculars trained on the ascending raptor. "I know—Hakanyi!"

Claire lowered hers to look at Victor. "What does that mean?"

"Fire," he said, still tied to the soaring hawk. "He's redder than she, and in the sun, he glows like fire." He cast a sideways glance to see her reaction.

❧ An Odd Bird ❧

"I love it!" she said. "But the name Hakanyi doesn't go with Big Red."

Victor weighed the argument on knitted brows. "We can give her a Cochiti name, too! In Cochiti, the word for "red" is "ku-khain."

"Ku-Khain," Claire whispered, releasing the word gently from her lips. "It's beautiful." Then she thought of the Cochiti name even yet withheld from her. "I bet your name is beautiful, too," she said expectantly, thinking he would surely tell her now.

But Victor ignored the overture. "What pies did Jerry bake today?" he said, turning away. "I'm hungry for pie. Let's get Patty and get back to the store."

Squabbling over whose shoulder should carry the pigeon, they stumbled along for some time until yanked by a harsh sound—the shout of an angry male voice: "And I mean NOW!"

Startled, they looked to one another in alarm. The shout came from the cabin, which lay about two hundred feet ahead, but it wasn't Jerry's voice. "Billy's father!" Claire cried, grabbing his arm and pulling him to the ground with her. "He might see us."

Crouching low, they scurried to conceal themselves beneath the thicket of a rose bush. It grew along the rutted lane leading to the cabin, the same lane that she and Jerry walked along on a sunny snow-crusted day to fetch Becky and Patty. "Patty!" The word flew from her mouth. Nothing more needed to be said. Both understood. Billy's father had sacrificed one pigeon as hawk bait and shot another from the air. What would he do to the innocent bird?

"We've got to find out what's going on in there," Claire said as she slipped free of her daypack for better mobility. Victor did the same. Then together, lying side by side, they

ꙮ Dangerous Drunk ꙮ

aimed binoculars toward the cabin. Into view came Clyde Hollow, stumbling into the fire ring, where he stood slouched, a pint of bourbon clutched in the hand dangling from his side.

"Git out here NOW!" growled the hapless man, swaying like a sapling in the wind.

Billy appeared in the doorway. Head hanging low and shoulders slumped, he dropped from the slightly raised doorsill to the ground like a weighted sack. And against his narrow chest, he clutched something: Patty. Claire tried to scramble free of the rambling bush, out into the open lane, but Victor grabbed her ankle.

"We have to sneak up on them," he said, twisting away to pull himself on elbows over the cold, wet ground to surface on the opposite side of the bush. Claire dove after, surfacing alongside where he sat on haunches, surveying the woodland. And in like fashion, dodging from one hideout to the next, they advanced on the cabin from behind, finally resting against its weathered backside. Through a window, they could see out the open door of the cabin to where Clyde still stood inside the fire ring, gesturing broadly, as if giving a lecture. But his only student was Billy, who sat on a tree stump, chin to his chest, stroking the pigeon clutched there.

"Unless you can shoot a live target"—Clyde lurched toward Billy, nearly falling into his lap, and plucked the pigeon from his son's chest—"well, then, you can't shoot t'all."

To Claire's horror, Clyde staggered backward with Patty firmly gripped in one hand.

"No clay pigeons allowed!" Clyde hooted, holding the pigeon over his head while his son swiped the air with a frantic hand to grab his father's wrist.

"Give it back!" Billy wailed like a child.

☙ An Odd Bird ☙

"Pigeons are for shooting," Clyde taunted, one arm swinging the bourbon pint and the other the pigeon. He was much amused with the game until Billy punched him, hard, in the stomach. From one hand the pint fell to the ground, and from the other, Patty flew into the air. Clyde stood suspended in a spasm of pain until dropping to his knees. Billy gaped in horror at what he had done, while Claire darted from behind the cabin, charging toward them.

"Get off Jerry's property!" She rushed to pick up the pint bottle and dashed it against a rock in the fire ring.

Billy pushed Claire. "You get out!" And she stumbled backward to the ground. Only then did he see Victor, who tackled his knees and knocked him down. Grunting, they rocked side to side, neither able to roll the other under. Claire watched this contest of wills, mindless of Clyde, who had recovered and stood, wobbling, where once he had slumped.

"You call that fighting?" He threw a hand toward them in disgust, nearly losing his balance. The boys instantly broke apart to watch Clyde shuffle past, heading toward the cabin. He wore a red flannel shirt, unbuttoned, over a faded, paint-stained navy T-shirt. He groped for something hidden behind the flung-wide cabin door. "But I can teach you a thing or two." And he hoisted a rifle, barrel up. "Now git over here and let me 'splain some things."

"We're not staying here!" shrieked Claire. "You're drunk!" And turning her back on Clyde, she grabbed Victor's arm. "Come on!"

Rising to his feet, Victor looked to his estranged friend. "Let's get out of here."

But Clyde answered for his red-faced and breathless son. "Billy ain't going anywhere." Into this tense scene dashed

❧ Dangerous Drunk ✥

Sammy, swaggering with the enthusiasm of a long deer chase through the woods.

"Let him talk a bit," Victor urged quietly, reluctant to leave Billy alone with his father.

"A bit," Claire said, more as a challenge than a surrender, while Sammy bounded playfully around them.

29
Sitting Target

The rifle casually leaning against his shoulder, Clyde barked orders like an army sergeant, telling them all to "sit for a lesson on life." While the boys scurried, each to a tree stump used as seats around the fire ring, Claire lingered too long by Sammy, leashed now to the cabin's door latch.

"Don't rile me, girl," Clyde said in an almost pleading voice, which scared her terribly. Scooting to the closest seat, she could see his bloodshot eyes searching for a memory in his skull.

"Hey, where's my pint?"

Billy was quick to blame Claire. "She threw it against those rocks, Pop—didn't ya see?"

The rifle slipped abruptly from his shoulder, through his groping hands, and smashed onto the ground. "Threw it against rocks?" Clyde seemed confused. Then, as if doused with cold water, he looked up, alert for the first time, and shot his glazed eyes to Claire.

"You—you hit me in the head with a rock!"

She stood, shouting back. "You only NOW recognize me?"

Victor jumped from his seat to pull her back down. "Don't make him mad."

But Claire bounced back up as Clyde strode closer, squinting at her. "It was you that stole my trophy buzzard!"

"You shot Mr. Buteo!" Claire shouted fearlessly. "And I'll report you for it!"

"YOU," he bellowed with rage, "will do what I say!" and pushed her back down onto the stump.

✥ Sitting Target ✤

Startled by the assault, Claire stayed seated, suddenly meek, as Clyde twisted away.

"You kids got no respect! Who's the add-dult here? I'm the add-dult. You list'n ta me!" And on this theme, he ranted for some minutes, until stumbling over the rifle. Picking it up, he slung it over his shoulder, inspired to begin a new rant. "My own flesh"—he threw a limp arm in Billy's direction—"don't do what I tell 'em! Won't go huntin'! Won't do nothin'! Gettin' that eye out turned him into a sissy."

Billy flew from his seat in protest. "I'm no sissy!" he screamed, trembling with pent-up rage. His face blazing red, Billy plowed into his father, grabbing for the rifle. "I'll show you," Billy grunted, wrestling for what Clyde now clasped with a fierce grip.

"Get off, you fool!" Clyde shook him loose with a violent thrust that sent the boy tumbling backward between two stumps to slam against the cabin. Whining, Sammy sniffed Billy as Victor watched, horrified. But Billy dashed through the cabin door, to sulk alone inside. Warily, Claire and Victor turned back toward Clyde, who still stood huffing from the exertion. For moments they watched him muttering to himself, pacing about and scouring the ground.

"Where's my pint?" he asked, exasperated.

Victor shot an anxious glance toward Claire, who knew not to utter a word. For some minutes they listened as Clyde muttered to himself. He seemed shrouded in darkness despite the shimmering afternoon sky. Stumbling, he sank onto a stomp to examine the loose sole of his shoe, letting the rifle fall to the ground. Victor and Claire ducked and shrieked against the potential blast, drawing Clyde's attention again. Their presence appeared to confuse and annoy him. "Git inside!" he barked, to assert some control. Rising from the ground, Claire caught a glimpse of Patty, in plain view, perched atop the outhouse. Victor, too, saw the pretty bird. Both dropped their heads and hurried into the cabin while Sammy, unleashed from the door handle, sniffed the area for new scents.

Inside, one window on each wall framed the fading afternoon. All were open to the outside air, with only sagging shutters to close out the cold. But neither the brisk April air nor afternoon light seemed to penetrate the small enclosure, now stuffed with four people. Claire and Victor sat on the floor against the wall opposite the door, closed against Sammy. Clyde sank onto the cot with an exaggerated sigh of exhaustion and pulled up his legs to lie down. Billy swiped the rifle from its resting place, barrel up, against the wall.

"Put down that rifle, you fool," said Clyde.

"Don't tell me what to do!" Billy shouted, roused once again. "I'm no sissy, and I can shoot better than you."

"Since when?"

"I've shot target with you!" Billy screamed.

Clyde suddenly sat up. "Lookey there," he said. "That pigeon's back."

Strutting along the windowsill behind Billy was Patty.

Claire was the first to act, lunging upward and screaming in a pitch that would scare a devil, causing the bird to take flight. But the pigeon didn't fly far enough away, perching on a low limb in a chestnut oak, only fifty feet away. Attempting to scramble through the window to charge the tree, Claire was grabbed about the middle by Clyde, who pulled her back.

"Hey, you can't grab her!" yelled Victor and began pounding on the arm clutching Claire in restraint. And in a twisting tangle of fury, the three spun off from the window, crashing across the room until colliding with and collapsing onto the cot, which crumbled beneath their weight.

❧ Sitting Target ❧

Billy stood by the window, watching Patty, as he raised the rifle slowly to his shoulder. "I'll show him who can shoot," he muttered, taking aim. But a fast-sweeping shadow, pressing hard upon the pigeon, caused her to plummet from the branch, where lethal talons closed on empty air.

The hawk had dived through a wide opening in the tree toward a single naked branch upon which Patty had patiently perched, like a gift. But in the instant before sinew and claw closed on her body, the pigeon plunged toward the ground, escaping death. The hawk swung upward toward the cabin, banking hard before the open window and Billy.

Billy stood stunned. He alone witnessed the spectacle, the others still groping about the floor. And just as he turned excitedly with the news, something drew him back. The hawk, a huge red-tail, returned to perch upon the very branch vacated by Patty. Transfixed, Billy stared at the hawk, whose chest was marked with a crimson cross, like a bull's-eye, inviting the bullet. And that's when he knew. "The trophy hawk," he whispered in awe. Directly before him, only fifty feet away, sat the hawk his father had hunted for years—all he had to do was raise the gun and pull the trigger.

Billy's movements became urgent because someone would soon notice and try to stop him. He hoisted the .22, nestled its butt into the crevice of his shoulder, and aimed the scope onto the crimson cross. As he fingered the trigger, the gaze of the raptor connected with his own through the spotting scope. He saw her eyes blaze . . . and loosened his finger. From the side he was pushed and knocked off balance.

"She's mine!" Clyde screeched, grabbing the rifle as Billy stumbled sideways. And as Clyde aimed, anticipating her upward lift, Big Red dove to the ground beneath a blasting shot. Uninjured, she scurried, while Clyde re-aimed, determined this time not to miss. "I got you this time," he said, an instant before Billy shoved him hard. And as the two fell, Big Red lifted from the ground, flying through the hole in the chestnut oak and up into the trees.

From the floor, Claire had helplessly watched the struggle between father and son. Everything had happened so quickly. The sound of the rifle blasts had caused her body to go limp. But Victor pulled her upward, clutching her waist and towing her on shuffling feet toward the door. Outside, at its base, Sammy scratched, frantic to get in. With the opening door, he plowed through, nearly knocking them over again. But on steadier feet, Claire led her dog outside while Victor returned for Billy, climbing off his sprawling father. Victor did not assist him but instead grabbed the rifle from the floor.

"What are you doing with that rifle?" demanded Billy, rising quickly to his feet.

Victor headed directly to the door. "I'm taking it away."

"No, you won't!" cried Billy, lunging toward the door.

But Victor was out and trotting after Claire and Sammy. "You can have it when we get back."

Billy looked to his father, grunting to sit up, and then to the trees, wherein the others had disappeared. "Pop, I'll be back later."

30
Cryptic Answers

In the days following, Claire hounded Jerry to confess that he was a wizard. She needed to believe that the old man could protect her family from people such as Clyde Hollow. The police had issued a warrant against him for illegally detaining three adolescents and discharging a weapon while drunk. But the officers sent to arrest him found only an empty cabin. Clyde's unknown whereabouts caused Claire significant grief, for she no longer felt safe in the woods. And it was spring—the best time to see and hear the return of the warblers.

According to Helen Whiner, broadcasting her views to whomever would listen, her good-for-nothing nephew was long gone. He had stolen money from her with which to flee. The police were of similar mind, but Claire took no comfort from these conclusions. One week had passed and still she would not go alone into her beloved woods, nor would her mother allow it. Only with Jerry were she and Sammy permitted to roam their usual haunts.

Because it was spring, Jerry agreed to take Claire out each morning before school. This morning a dusting of snow covered the greening grass. They headed outside under a widening blue sky pierced by the rising sun. The cold air pulsed with the sweet, shrill songs of hundreds of birds—among them goldfinch, robins, and song sparrows. And through the harmonious din could be heard the call of a single phoebe, the light-gray-and-white flycatcher that says his own name: phoebe, phoebe, phoebe.

Amid a riot of birdsong, they climbed a winding deer trail through mature hemlocks, padded by pine needles, where an ovenbird screeched its challenge: TEACHER, TEACHER, TEACHER! Unlike typical warblers, the ovenbird spends much of its time on the ground and so is difficult to see, but Claire spotted him even so, a reddish-brown bird scratching for insects in the leaf litter.

The two proceeded in this way to various habitats preferable to different bird species within the woods. And in forty-five minutes they had identified no fewer than twenty-three birds, including those in their yard. They headed back, waiting below the mighty oak for Sammy to join them. "You know," Claire said, stepping over the tree roots, "if you tell me more about being a wiz"—she drew back the word, rolling her eyes—"guardian of the woods or whatever, I'll tell you something about me."

"Sounds fair," he said, surprising her.

"Really?" Searching his blue-gray eyes for hint of a hoax, she added quickly, "You have to go first."

"Okay, but the bus will be along in about six minutes."

Claire stomped against the restriction—her interrogation undermined before it even began! Of all the questions she wanted answered, she could think of only one, and it not the most important. "How is it that you can come and go without people seeing you? Like when you get Moon Doggy or clean the pigeon loft and Helen never knows." These words spoken, she instantly remembered the most important questions, which she nearly shouted: "Did you know about me before we met? Did you set up our meetings?"

Jerry shook his head against the onslaught. "Whoa, little girl. One thing at a time."

❧ Cryptic Answers ❦

Claire could tell he was stalling. "No! Tell me, please! I have a right to know."

Sammy charged up from the water hole, wet and happy, adding yet another distraction. Jerry dodged the sheepdog about to shake off the water. "Come on," he said, "I'll tell you as we go."

She raced to his side, willing him with her heart to speak quickly.

"It's true," he said, eyes following the path over which they walked. "I've known about you for a long time."

Claire stopped; though he urged her onward, she remained immobile.

"You're no typical kid, Claire," he said. "And I know your secret." He looked behind to the bus turning the curve on the road above them. "But now's not the time or place."

Hurrying ahead to meet the bus, she called back: "Then after school—when you air the birds."

On the bus rides to and from school, Claire and Victor took turns interpreting what Jerry's cryptic answers had meant. Claire found all her suspicions confirmed. "He said, 'And I know your secret.' How in the world could he know that?" She paused as if to allow him time for a response but quickly filled it. "I'll tell you how: He reads minds, reads my journal, or listens to us talk."

Victor, however, refused to be persuaded. "But what secret did he mean? You're assuming it's about you and the birds." Before either could convince the other, the bus stopped to drop off Victor, leaving Claire alone to anticipate her upcoming meeting.

31
Into the *Now*

Jerry stood by the chicken house with Sammy seated calmly beside him. Running across the yard, Claire heaved from her shoulders the book bag, which fell to the soppy ground above the pond. Here, during the wet spring, groundwater seeping into the turf created deep puddles. Though they soaked her feet, she cared not. She thought of only one thing: the truth.

Before she could speak, Jerry opened the wood-framed wire door into the fenced run and waved her in. "Let me show you something." Expecting to fight Sammy back, she looked behind to find him still seated and seemingly disinterested.

"What's wrong with Sammy?" she said, distracted as she stepped into a whirlwind of fowl, flapping and squawking in long-awaited welcome.

"Nothing," said Jerry. "We've got an understanding."

While Claire puzzled this out, Jerry led her to the single step of a low, narrow doorway. She ducked into a clean but cramped and heated space. Directly across were cubbies for his roosting birds but, oddly, some were occupied by visitors. More oddly still, not all were birds. A cottontail rabbit curled in one and three tiny red squirrels in another. Scanning a row of cubbies above, she found, to her utter amazement, a northern saw-whet, a miniature owl that she could cradle in her hand—dare she touch it! Huge golden eyes stared at her in alarm, their black pupils dilating.

"Jerry," she said urgently, "why do you have an owl?"

"His wing is broken. He's healing."

"And these others?"

❧ Into the *Now* ❧

"Rabbit got hit with BB shot; red squirrels lost their mother. Don't know how."

Though hard to do, Claire moved her gaze from the owl to Jerry. "So this is what you do as a guardian?"

"Mostly." He turned to head outside. Claire took one last look at the adorable owl, like two puff balls, one atop the other. She kissed her fingertip and lowered it slowly to tap his head.

Outside, they took the path leading up to the pasture. Becky scampered ahead, and Patty flew within the hillside cherry trees. Claire wanted to know everything about the animals in the chicken house: Did her mother know? Did he tend them often? Could she help? But each question took her farther from the most urgent question. She finally returned to this question as they trod the gentle, winding incline around the hill shoulder. Atop was a bench, a long plank of rough oak resting on a foundation of cinder blocks. Here they sat to look down over the hollow that held the house, pond, and meadow. All was bordered by the adjacent woodland trimmed with a row of high white pines. The sun, sinking in the sky behind them, cast a gilded sheen over everything.

"That blue heron I told you about," said Jerry, lifting one bushy brow, "he did more than give me fish." His hazel eye dared her to guess.

Claire sat up straighter, exhaling in expectation.

"He spoke to me from some place beyond the mind."

She gawked at him in disbelief.

"Not with words. Words and thoughts are mental. He connected with me at a deeper level."

Claire struggled to understand. "Do you mean the subconscious?"

"No, I don't mean that, either. I was conscious, all right."

"Well, what then?" she said with exasperation.

"He showed me myself."

Claire sprang up from the bench to stomp her foot. "Tell me something that makes sense!"

Jerry spoke soothingly. "Whenever I looked at Stan long enough, eye to eye, he took me somewhere."

Claire recognized the experience. "Like you were going inside his eyes?"

"Yeah, like that. Everything would disappear, but I could feel his presence."

"That's happened to me!" She jumped up and down, speaking with large hand gestures. "At first everything vanishes, and then I feel like I'm going to slide into their eyes."

"It's happened more than once?"

"A few times," she said, looking to him for interpretation, but his response was too slow in the coming. "But you—you've gone inside?"

Jerry stood, overlooking the hillside for Becky's whereabouts. She pecked below among the high tussocks of grass. "I went somewhere, but not a physical place." He turned back to Claire. "No, that's not right; let me explain better. My physical body didn't go anywhere; my awareness went somewhere."

"Where?"

"I think I went into the *Now*."

32
All That Live

With spring migration at its peak, Jerry and Claire spent every dawn scouting for warblers. They especially sought the cerulean, named for the deep sky-blue feathers of his head and back. For two breeding seasons, Claire hadn't seen the blue and white bird or heard its buzzy, trilling song. The tiny songbird was in decline. Its wintering grounds in the high Andean forests of South America were being cleared for coffee plantations while its breeding forests in North American were being cleared for development. Humanity was crowding him out.

Today, while Sammy romped ahead, Jerry led the way across the pasture toward the mighty white oak and creek. Filling the thin morning air was the manic music of songbirds. From treetop and bush, male birds whistled or trilled to attract mates or to warn against trespass. To find the cerulean, they would seek out the warbler's preferred nesting and foraging trees. "There's a good stand of sugar maple in the hollow below my cabin," he said, clutching the straps of his daypack.

Crossing the creek, they headed westward, where the forest canopy closed overhead, a green trembling roof filled with birdsong. Even while Jerry quizzed her on the names of different trees, Claire was preoccupied with the cerulean, holding his image in her mind. If the bird were anywhere near, she would bring him in. But should she confide this ability to Jerry? As if reading her mind, he turned abruptly, propping his hand against the trunk of a chestnut oak. "So, go ahead. Ask."

Twisting her lips, she studied him. More than ever he looked like a wizard, his salt and pepper beard again full and his hair thick and kinky. "Do you really know my secret?"

"That I do." He wore his most wizardly self-satisfied expression.

"What is it, then?" she said, challenging him.

"You, Claire, can do what few can." He took his hand from the tree trunk to place on her shoulder as his bushy brows lifted in announcement: "You can go into the *Now*."

Disappointed, she dropped her head. "That's not my secret; and, besides, I can't."

"You can," he persisted, "when you want to."

She pushed sulkily past him. "Even *if*—that's not my secret," she said, striding rapidly onward while he stood rooted.

"There's a reason birds are drawn to you," he called. His words, like a snag across the path, caused her to stumble. She turned quickly. He did know!

"Birds come to you like an old friend because you are one. You spend much time with them in the *Now*."

Though intriguing, this declaration made no sense to Claire. Yet Jerry refused to explain until they reached their destination. So they pushed eagerly onward, descending gradually toward the creek, which could be heard, if not seen, through the trees. Here the woodland opened into a wide glade of century-old sugar maples. "See how wide and full these are?" Jerry said, stepping briskly beneath the closest to look happily up into its leafy boughs. "No competition. These were cultivated after loggers had cleared the land. And browsing deer have kept the space open." At mention of deer, Claire spotted the tawny coat of a doe deep within the glade. She blinked and then saw another, closer still, within a cluster of yellow birch.

"Jerry," she whispered, casting him a sideway glance, but he was moving toward the birch trees. She cried out to stop him: "A deer!"

Over his shoulder he called back, "I know her," and casting his hand added, "these others, too." Claire turned quickly behind to see, close by, two doe and a young buck. The buck dipped his head, crowned with tender antlers, to browse upon the high switchgrass. The doe blinked lazily, without alarm. Claire, however, felt a bit unnerved with the nearness of the large ruminants. She dashed to Jerry's side as he approached the birch trees where a single deer stood drinking water from a ground spring.

"What about Sammy?" she whispered, grabbing his arm. "He'll chase after them."

Squatting to cup his hand in the cold water for a drink, Jerry said, "Don't worry; he's preoccupied." He led her up a grassy slope through wild rose and barberry bushes. "I've a surprise for you," he said, pushing through a high wall of honeysuckle that thickened the air with heavy, sweet fragrance. Claire shut her eyes to plow through the poking stems and opened them to something unexpected: a rectangular space, like a large room carpeted in emerald moss, but with walls of honeysuckle. Jerry stood at its center smiling expectantly.

"This is my secret hideaway," he said, clasping and squeezing his hands in delight. "It's the foundation of a stone house from two-hundred years back. And look," he stepped sprightly aside to reveal what lay behind him, a low table of weathered oak boards and bench seats. "Mike and me built it to use right here." He dropped his backpack onto it like an anchor. "A place to hide from Helen."

Open mouthed, Claire drifted around the space scanning for any breach in the floral walls filled with bees. "This is so cool," she said, plopping onto a bench while Jerry unpacked their breakfast. "But couldn't you hide at your cabin?"

"Nah. That woman was a hound dog; she'd sniff us out every time." He handed her half a bagel with cream cheese and an apple. "No, we had to find someplace to smoke our pipes in peace."

While they ate, Jerry fulfilled his earlier promise to explain about her time spent with birds in the *Now*. He said that unlike most people, animals were connected to the *Now*. They lived each moment in the present, not preoccupied with hopes for the future or regrets about the past. He said that every time she focused intently on a bird, she occupied the present moment with that bird, which meant that they were both in the *Now*.

"Is that all?" she said, crestfallen, the rosy apple stalled in its trajectory toward her mouth. "I thought you meant we would be together in some special place, another dimension or something." Before he could respond, she doubled her complaint. "And that doesn't explain why everything around me and the bird seems to disappear—"

He raised his hand like a crossing guard against further grievance. "I'm getting to that, Missy. Just listen."

She obeyed with a big chomp of the apple, at least, for the time it would take to chew.

"When you're present, nothing exists but the object of your focus. Think of a gymnast somersaulting on one of those beams. They do that in the *Now*. They see nothing else and think nothing else."

Claire swallowed and sighed, demonstrating her impatience.

"The difference with you," he said, eyes popping, "is that the birds, who are always in the *Now*, are guiding you in more deeply."

"More deeply?"

"Yeah, really deep."

"Something like a trance?" she asked.

"Exactly."

"But why?"

Jerry slapped his lap and stood to speak as instructor to student.

"You and me, Claire, are no ordinary folk." He squinted at her as he often did. "But all my life, I thought I was the only one. In fact, I thought I understood and was fulfilling my purpose."

"Helping animals?"

"Helping all that live. But then you moved into the Kelly house, and the woods came alive with chatter. And it didn't take long for me to find out." With a great exhalation of breath, Jerry plopped down beside her and cupped one of her hands into his own.

"Claire, my real purpose is to train you, just like Stan trained me. But I won't be the only one." He gripped her hand more tightly. "Much is expected of you, now and throughout your life, to help the birds of this world."

33

The Hatchling

Twenty feet above the hawks' nest, Claire lay stomach down, groping a broad, sturdy maple limb. "Can you see them yet?" Victor called from below. He stood beneath the huge tree, whose rippling roots dug beneath the sandstone of the outcrop called the Finger.

"Not yet," she said shakily.

The apprehension in her voice alerted Victor to the danger, if belatedly. "Maybe you should come down," he said, watching Claire wiggle over the maple's stout arm, which extended into the open, groundless space beyond the rock shelf. Behind her, the sun was high in the morning sky.

"Just a bit more." Grunting, she inched forward. "I can see it!"

"Be careful!"

Claire swung her legs downward to straddle the limb like a horse, her torso tight against the bark. Slowly she pushed upward, concentrating on balance. Then she pulled binoculars to her eyes.

"Three eggs, Victor!"

"Great—now get down."

"Wait! One of the eggs . . . it's moving."

Victor left his station by the tree trunk to climb onto the outcrop, hurrying to its edge that faced the adjacent outcrop, the Fist. Always before, they had viewed the nest through binoculars from the distance of the Fist. But today Claire wanted to view it from above to see down inside the nest for eggs.

"A chick is hatching!" she cried, legs swinging.

"Watch that you don't fall!" he hollered. "You're out over the ledge!"

"I won't fall!" she shouted, laughing at his concern. Since talking with Jerry about the blue heron and Big Red (now Ku-Khain), she felt liberated, even invincible. But Victor didn't hear her, for a mighty rush of dark wings, wider by far than his own shoulders, careened overhead. He ducked, hiding his head from the hawk, whose avenging scream bore into his skull.

Through a hole in the leaves of the tree, Claire could see the male hawk fly out over the Fist and then bank to head again toward the Finger.

Get off the outcrop!" she screeched from her perch, but Victor stayed huddled. "Get up!" she screamed, nearly bouncing off the limb, but Victor still huddled. Again, the angry raptor screeched, before dive-bombing him. Then Claire lost balance and her hip slipped. To keep from falling, she flung forward, chest against the limb, heart pounding. A downward glance brought the outcrop into view, where Billy, looking nervously into the sky, was pulling Victor up by the hand. For some seconds she lay, stomach against the limb, hugging it with her arms and thighs. Her palms felt sweaty. How long could she hold on? Cheek pressed against rough bark, she inched backward, every muscle awash in adrenaline. Finally, her tailbone hit the trunk. Pushing upward, she twisted around to embrace it. She was safe! Dropping to the ground, she absorbed the impact in her knees and collapsed.

"Get up," said Victor, appearing above her. "Are you all right?" He grabbed her by the hand, but she collapsed on wobbly legs; the fright of falling had drained her of all strength and focus. She watched as Victor's head popped up under her arm. The novelty of it took all her attention until she felt herself rising, weightless. Only then did she look to see another head covered by mousy, oily hair, growing out of her other armpit.

No one spoke as Victor and Billy carted Claire through the mountain laurel, blooming in creamy pink petals with veins of deeper pink. But the only scent she smelled was that of Billy's body odor. When clear of the laurel, the three headed to a small stand of hemlock, where all sank onto soft needles.

"What's he doing here?" Claire said to Victor, tone indignant despite her enemy's aid. She scooted away from Billy and his body odor. "Were you following us?"

Billy shook his head and rose to leave until Claire cried, "Wait! I'm sorry."

Billy turned back, looking at her with a measure of gratitude. And in his earnest gaze, she suddenly could see her own inner self—a hurtful, wicked girl, who had wished him only harm. Images of Billy with his face stamped by disappointment, hurt, or fear filled her mind, all images of someone other than a bully. Furtively watching him, she stood, brushing hemlock needles from the seat of her pants. She waited on the two, unsure how to behave in this new world where Billy was a person just like her, just like Victor.

Heading through the woods, Claire walked behind the boys, waiting for a chance to join their jovial talk, which had just turned to something about "great news." Billy goaded Victor to guess his news. After several attempts, Victor stopped to jump atop the flat surface of a petrified tree stump. "Just tell me already!"

"Let me stand there," Billy said, crowding Victor off. "I need a stage for this kind of news."

❧ The Hatchling ❦

Claire stood alongside Victor in a sudden brisk wind that everywhere rustled the green leaves of spring, a fanfare of sorts for Billy's great news.

"Okay." He waved his hand like a magician. "You thought that we burned up in the Martian atmosphere because of me." He took a deep breath. "Guess what? After us, the next crew burned up, too. And then the one after that and the one after that!" He punched the air with his fist. "Turns out the game's program was at fault!" He stooped, hands to knees, eager to see Victor's reaction.

"Everybody burned up?" Victor said, still trying to understand the implications. But Claire already understood, and her smile quickly faded as Billy jumped down to Victor.

"Yes! Don't you see? We get to try again! Everybody does. But we're still in first place orbiting Mars!"

Victor shot upward. Soon they were punching one another, frantic in their joy. Claire at first watched the spectacle with a sour expression. Yet their giddy antics were too funny. And suddenly she too jumped up and down, each boy pulling her by an arm into an unbroken chain of delight. Exhausting their excitement, the three broke again into separate selves, marching single file along a narrow deer path cut diagonally across the steep hillside.

Victor reached for Claire's arm to hold her back a moment while Billy walked ahead. "Tahwach, I forgot to tell you something." And into her ear he whispered his Cochiti name as the screech of a red-tailed hawk filled the air.

About the Author

P.K. Butler is a Pennsylvania-based author of children's books. She earned a Master of Art degree in English from Pennsylvania State University and thereafter pursued a teaching career in higher education. Butler, who lives in Gettysburg, is an active birder and walker, always on the lookout for new trails to explore with her two big dogs, Rosie and Henry. Learn more about her and the real-life animals she has fictionalized within her trilogy *Of the Wing* at **pkbutler.com**

Dear Reader,

If you enjoyed this book, please leave a review on Amazon (or Goodreads). I read every review, and they help new readers discover my books. Thank you!

Made in the USA
Las Vegas, NV
02 June 2022